I0651729

Anonymous

The Apocalyptic Drama

Anonymous

The Apocalyptic Drama

ISBN/EAN: 9783337344818

Printed in Europe, USA, Canada, Australia, Japan

Cover: Foto ©Andreas Hilbeck / pixelio.de

More available books at **www.hansebooks.com**

THE

APOCALYPTIC DRAMA

"We have .. a .. sure word of prophecy, whereunto ye do
well that ye take heed, as unto a light that shineth in a dark
place. until the day dawn, and the day-star arise in your
hearts."—*2 Pet. 1:19.*

NEW YORK AND CHICAGO.
Fleming H. Revell Company
PUBLISHERS OF EVANGELICAL LITERATURE.

Entered According to Act of Congress in the Year 1891,
BY FLEMING H. REVELL COMPANY,
In the Office of Librarian of Congress at Washington.

GREETING :
"Unto all them that love his appearing."

THE APOCALYPTIC DRAMA.

GOOD AND EVIL.

"And the Lord God said, behold, the man has become as one of us, to know good and evil."* Alas, for man, that it has been so. He pays dearly for his knowledge. And, what is to be the end of it?—is now the all important question. The good and the evil are inseparable from us. They are within and without. They are mixed up, inexplicably mixed up; and their antagonism is intense. Must it ever be so? Is the strife inevitable? Is this the order, or rather, the disorder of the universe? Is it nature with her inexorable law—unalterable, everlasting; or is the evil destined to gain the ascendancy, and to assume the mastery? It seems the stronger of the two. "What I would, that do I not; but what I hate, that do I."† Is, then, this principle of evil to go on increasing in strength, untill mind and matter—all the universe—shall succumb to its power, and evil, and only evil, be the law of being? These questions are forcing themselves upon

* Gen. 3: 22.   † Rom. 7:15.

us. Neither our philosophy nor our science have as yet answered them; nor is there any prospect that they will ever be able to do so. If an answer come, it must be from the beyond—from the unseen, the spiritual. And we who bow before an all-wise Creator and governor of the universe, not only look to him for an answer to these questions, but we believe that he has already given it. His word, "the scriptures of truth," recognizes the existence in this world of these two conflicting principles. This word begins with an account of the way in which the evil was introduced; its every succeeding narrative is an unfolding of the irrepressible conflict between the two as antagonized principles; and it ends with the "mystery of iniquity" finished, sin cast out, and truth and righteousness triumphant.

THE STUDY OF PROPHECY.

To those who accept this word as a divine revelation, and who "keep those things which are written," this conflict and this consummation must be a subject of never-failing interest. There must be a desire on the part of all such to "look into these things," not, however, with idle curiosity. All scripture is given for our profit. Even in its hard sayings, and its mysteries, and its far-reach-ing prophecies, wrapped up in the language of type and symbol—even in these, there must be instruction, for they are a part of "all scripture." The question as to the propriety of searching into these hidden things has disturbed many devout minds, and has led to a neglect of the study of prophecy. And yet this question seems to have been anticipated and answered in the word itself. At the very outset, e. g., of the book of Revelation, and before a prophecy is uttered or a symbol used, a blessing is invoked on him "that readeth" and on them "that hear the words of this prophecy, and keep those things which are written therein."* And as the book begins, so does it end, with benediction on him who studies these mysteries. "Blessed is he that keepeth the sayings of the prophecy of this book."†

And let it be noted that nothing is said of *understanding*. The blessing is in hearing the words, and in keeping the things written in the heart, for warning, instruction, and hope. The wonderful things spoken concerning Jesus, and also by himself, were not understood by his mother: but we are told that she "kept" them, and "pondered them in her heart."‡ And there continues to be many things spoken by Jesus, or concern-

* 1:3.   † 22:7.   ‡ Lu. 2:19.

ing him, that we cannot now understand; but we can keep it in our hearts and ponder them. And this is what the Lord would have us do in regard to everything given us in his word. Prophecy is no exception. If there is much connected with it that is mysterious and beyond our present grasp, there is much more that is plain and simple, and within the reach of every docile mind willing to take God at his word. And it is these "things"—these fundamental facts—that lie on the very surface of scripture, and especially its prophetic portions, that we are to treasure up in our hearts.

Look at some of these things that the "sure word of prophecy"—prophecy used in its large sense of forth-telling—has revealed to us. The world that now is with in the power of the evil one.* The gospel is in it witnessing for Jesus, inviting, warning, and taking from among the Gentiles, a people for His name.† The evil element working in the world is eventually to culminate in the lawless one, who is to be energized by Satan: along with his appearing there is to be a great falling away in the church.‡ The Lord is to come again. He is to bring his saints with him.|| He is to put all enemies

*John 5:19.   † Acts 1:18. 15:14.   ‡ 2 Thess. 2:1-11
|| 1 Thess. 4:13 &c.

under his feet.* There will be a new heaven and a new earth. Old things are to pass away, all things are to become new.†

These are great truths, clearly stated, easy of comprehension, and well calculated to inspire hope, to awaken desire, to lift the thoughts above the things seen, to center the affections on things not seen, and to make the heart cry out—"Come, Lord Jesus, come quickly." Surely these are "sayings" to read, and to hear about, and to keep in the heart, and to ponder.

And so also of the things not so easy of comprehension. There are indeed, many such, and from the nature of these "sayings," it is to be expected. But let it be remembered that these are not forbidden things. They, too, are among the sayings of the book that are to be kept. Prophecies that are now understood were once inexplicable even to angels. Yet they desired to look into them, and were not chided for an irreverent curiosity.‡ Of things future, disciples asked: "Tell us, when shall these things be? And what the sign of thy coming, and the end of the world (age)?"§ The master's reply is prompt, and it meets all the demands of his questioners. Nor is there on the occasion a note of warning against a too inquisitive

*1 Cor. 15: 24-26. †Rev. 21. ‡1 Tit. 1:12. §Math. 24:3

spirit that would know things that are coming on the earth.

Such is the character of the sayings of the
book we propose considering.   They relate to
things that either have come, or are yet to
come.   And though there is much that is
sealed, and beside which we must write the ·
word *mystery*, yet their consideration is not
forbidden.   They, too, are among the sayings
to be heard, and read, and pondered.   We
know so much, that we can well afford to
exercise patience and wait for that which is
not plain. "At the end it shall speak and
not lie: though it tarry, wait for it."*   In
due time we shall walk with the master, and
our understandings shall be opened.   He will
himself be our teacher.   Beginning with
Moses and all the prophets, he will expound
unto us in all the scriptures the things concerning himself.   Meanwhile, disciples are
to keep all these things in their hearts, pro-
fiting by what they know, pondering over
what they cannot understand, and ever desiring and receiving more and more of the promised blessing.

THE OBJECT OF THE BOOK.

It has been in this spirit that the book of
Revelation has been studied by a few loving

* Heb. 2:3.

students of the word, and we send out some
of the results of our studies. What, another
book? Yes. More wild fancies to be con-
signed to the flames? Perhaps so. Many
and crude have been the interpretations given
to the words of this book. But what of that?
They have been in the line of the master's
command, and they have kept the fact of a
coming Christ before the world. Time has
corrected many of the misconceptions of the
past and will continue to do so. The very inad-
equacy of some of these conceptions, has stimulated others to a more intelligent study and
to more satisfactory results. Thus will it
be to the end, when the vision "shall speak,
and not lie," and the command is, "wait for
it." Now it is waiting for the vision, not in
the idleness of indifference, but in reading and
speaking often one to another concerning the
things that are written—it is in this spirit of
waiting, that our book has taken shape. We
make no claim to a solution of the mystery, or
indeed, of any of the mysteries of the book.
Far from it. It is an humble feeling after
truth, if haply we may find, be it only the
smallest fragment. If we do not throw light
on our subject, who shall say that another,
stimulated by our very dullness, may not receive inspiration, and so the church eventually be edified. Then will our little book have

accomplished its mission, and it can be assigned to the grave of forgetfulness.

In studying the Apocalypse, its structural character has occupied our attention more than exegesis; and our thoughts have been led in this direction from the examination of other prophecies. That our readers may be the better prepared to go along with us and to feel the force of the suggestions to be made, we must ask them to follow us in a brief outline of at least one of these prophecies.

DANIEL 9:24-29.

In our interpretation of prophecy we follow mainly those who are known as literalists. We regard Daniel's prophecy of the 70 weeks as an epitomized history of the world, from the rebuilding of Jerusalem, after the Babylonish captivity, to the second coming of the Lord. The 70 weeks, we are told, concern "thy people and thy holy city." The prophecy then in the strictest sense relates to Israel. And yet there is wrapped up in it of very necessity, the history, not of Israel only, but of the church and the world, and that to the end. When it speaks, it is of Israel. But there is a break, a long interval between its 69th week and its 70th. And here its silence is most instructive, for it sends you elsewhere with the inquiry

—what of this interval? It is here that much of previous prophecies, and of all that follows, whether spoken by the Lord or his disciples, falls into place. These prophecies break the silence and fill up what has been left unsaid by Daniel.

The Hebrew word here * translated "weeks" is the word that is used to denote a heptard or period of seven days. But it is claimed by most commentators that in the prophecy it stands for a longer period. It is thought that a week of years, and not of days, is intended. And this is common sense. To make these 70 weeks, weeks of days, is to assign a period of less than one year and a half (1 ½) for the whole course of the prophecy. This clearly was not the intent of the Spirit.

Regarding the prophecy then as speaking of weeks of years, the whole period designated amounts to 490 years, and is divided into three portions:

(a),	7 weeks,	(V. 25),	49 years.
(b), 62	" "	" "	434 "
(c),	1 " "	(V. 27),	7 " "
	70 " "		490 " "

Verse 24 tells us what is to be accomplished when the whole period of 70 weeks has run its course, viz., the finishing of transgression, etc.

* Dan. 9:24.

In v. 25 we learn that "from the going forth of the commandment to restore and to build Jerusalem, unto Messiah the Prince, shall be seven weeks, and three score and two weeks." Seven weeks, i. e., 49 years, will be consumed in the rebuilding of the city; and 62 weeks, i. e., 434 years, will elapse from that time to the cutting off of Messiah. After this event the city and sanctuary are destroyed. 49 and 434=483 years. There yet remains one week, or seven years of the prophecy unfulfilled, to make up the whole period of 490 years.

Up to this point there is much unanimity in interpretation, but just here there is divergence. What of this week? We concur with those who hold that after the cutting off of Messiah at the close of the 69th week, the further fulfilment of the prophecy is stayed. It stops short within a week of its entire fulfilment, and that last week still waits to run its course.

In v. 26 we read that Messiah shall "be cut off, but not for himself." The margin reads, and so also the R. V.—"And shall have nothing,"—i. e., instead of a kingdom which he sent his fore-runner to announce, and which he came to establish, he has nothing. Israel would none of him. They disallowed his claims, rejected his person, and refused

him his throne. He is cast out of the vineyard, and he is sent away empty.

Consequent upon this rejection, "the
people of the prince that shall come shall destroy the city and the sanctuary; and the end
thereof (i. e. of this destruction) shall be
with a flood, and even unto the end shall be
war; desolations are determined." (R. V.)
The idea seems to be this: This destruction
of their city and temple is only the beginning
of this new controversy that Jehovah God
will now have with his people on account of
their rejection of their Messiah. Indignation
and wrath will be poured out upon them a
tremendous and resistless flood, and it will be
prolonged "many days."* Desolations are
determined even unto the end of this divine
war. "The end". This is a point of time
frequently referred to by Daniel.† It is found
also in the N. T. scriptures.‡ From the destruction of the city to "the end"—a point
in time determined on in divine councils, but
not yet revealed—desolations are determined
upon Irsael.

Now observe that the cutting off of Messiah
brings us to the close of the 69th week of the
prophecy. There remains one more week to
complete the 70. The predictions of v. 26
concern the destruction of the city, which is

* Hos. 3:4.   † 12:4, 6, 9, 13.   ‡ Matt. 13:40, 24:3, 13, 14.

the beginning of a war that is to last to " the end." This (to " the end ") is an indefinite period that has been running on for over eighteen centuries, and " the end " is not yet, whereas this particular prophecy calls for only one more week of seven years. These prophecies therefore concerning these determined desolations can have no relation to this week.

Then again, these prophecies of v. 26 relate to divine wrath poured on Israel, whereas the 70 weeks portend blessings. Look at them. V. 24: " Seventy weeks are determined upon thy people, and upon thy holy city, to finish the transgression, and to make an end of sins, and to make reconciliation for iniquity, and to bring in everlasting righteousness, and to seal up the vision and prophecy, and to anoint the most holy." All this is just the reverse of "desolations are determined " (v. 26). Surely these gracious purposes await their fulfilment, and the 70th week of the prophecy is yet to dawn on Israel and the world in the fulness of its blessedness.

We are then forced to the conclusion that there has been an interruption in the onward movement of this prophecy. Its further fulfillment is clearly arrested at the cutting off of Messiah; and its 70th or last week awaits

its accomplishment.　In the hiatus thus created, we are living.

This interpretation is important in its bearing on the suggestions to be proposed in our study of the Apocalypse.　We must therefore ask for it further consideration.

Our theory is, that of the 70 weeks of Daniel's prophecy, 69 have met their fulfilment. One week remains to run its course.　There has therefore been an interruption in the continuity of the prophecy.　At the time of the cutting off of Messiah there was a break.　It has lasted now through nineteen centuries, and it will continue to the time of "the end", when again the prophecy will resume its course, and the announcements connected with its last heptard will have their fulfillment.　Is this fanciful?　Is it trifling with the word of God by an attempted accommodation to our preconceived notions?　Or does the prophecy itself necessitate such an interpretation, and does the analogy of scripture authorize it?　Let us see.

(a) We claim that the prophecy itself necessitates this view.　It concerns Israel, and Israel only.　Daniel has been confessing the sins of his people, and has been presenting his supplication for the holy mountain of his God (v. 20).　While he is yet speaking the man Gabriel comes to him to give him understanding. He tells him: "Seventy weeks are determined upon *thy people*, and upon *thy holy city* (v. 24). The prophecy then relates to Israel and to their city, and to them only. In his explanations the announcing angel reaches a point where people and city are not (v. 26). "The people of the prince that shall come, shall destroy the city and the sanctuary." They cease to be. Israel is no longer a nation. Their house has been left unto them desolate.* And this is to be their condition for "many days".† Of necessity therefore, all through these "many days" of desolation, the onward course of the prophecy toward its fulfilment must be arrested. The one week that remains concerns them as much as did the 69 that are passed. What remains of the prophecy to be fulfilled (its last heptard), must therefore continue in this state of suspense until the nation, and city, and sanctuary, have existence again. Their existence is a necessity to the requirements of the prophecy. Its fulfillment is suspended because they are not. In the interim, we have the history of the "scattered" people, and the destroyed city, in the closing statements of v. 26. It is a war of divine judgments against them because they have rejected and cut off their Messiah. The

---

* Matt. 23:38. † Hos. 3:4.

vineyard has been taken from them and given to others.* Their house has been left unto them "desolate;" it still remains for them, but desolate.† And they "shall be led captives into all nations, and Jerusalem shall be trodden down of the Gentiles, until the times of the Gentiles be fulfilled."‡

(*b*) This view of the prophecy is further necessitated by its relation to other prophecies. The word of God is a unit. Even when not so expressed, there is always implied a connection and dependence of parts with parts. Scripture is to be compared with scripture. One statement is to be contrasted with another, and the harmony of the whole is thus to be adjusted. And the prophetic portions are no exceptions to this rule. Every prophecy has relations of more or less importance with those that have preceded it. In seeking interpretations therefore, these mutual relations and dependencies are important factors. Many other prophecies concerning Israel had preceded the one we are considering. Its uninterrupted fulfillment to "the end" must therefore depend upon the manner in which the conditions of these prior prophecies shall be carried out. E. g. In Deut. 18: 18, 19, we find the promise of a coming prophet like unto Moses. Along

* Matt. 21:33, &c. † Matt. 23:38. ‡ Lu. 21:24.

with this announcement is a warning against an ungracious reception of this prophet, and threatened punishment should they not hearken to his words. And this was the very thing that Israel did. They refused to hearken to the words of this prophet, and they rejected their Messiah. But all scripture must be fulfilled, and in its fulfillment must harmonize. Hence it is that just at this point in Daniel's prophecy—the cutting off of Messiah—the two prophecies touch each other, and there is need of adjustment. The fulfillment of the entire 70 weeks is dependent upon what Israel will do with a prophet whom Moses has announced. If they will hearken unto him, then the 70 weeks can move on in their fulfillment, and the conclusion of the last week will find Israel in possession of all the blessings announced in v. 24. But Israel in the exercise of the freedom of the will, rejected the prophet, and therefore Daniel's prophecy had to give way to the threatened punishments of the prior prophecy. Daniel's last week has been suspended until Moses' forewarned judgments are executed.* Many other prophecies have a similar bearing upon this one of Daniel's that we are considering, e. g., Lev. 26. Deut. 28. Josh. 23:15, 16. Is. 1:19, 20.

*Acts 3:22, etc.

It is thus apparent that the dependence of this prophecy on others necessitates the suspension of the fulfillment of its last week in order that the unity and harmony of scripture may be maintained.

(c) And this conditional feature in a book so full of strong and positive state ments must not surprise us. The warnings, counsels, commands and promises of scripture are addressed to intelligent and free agents, and God never loses sight of this fact. In proportion as he gives liberty to the creature, he limits himself. "If ye will harken unto me," etc. "If ye will obey my voice," etc. "I would . . . ye would not." "Ye will not come to me that ye may have life."* Such is the conditional element that runs through the whole of scripture. The prophecies are no exception. If this element is not always expressed it is always implied. And hence we find many prophecies marked with the peculiarity that we are claiming for these 70 weeks of Daniel. Look for instance at the commission given to Moses to lead the children of Israel into Canaan. It was a short journey from Egypt to Canaan. A few weeks at most could have accomplished it. So far as the record shows it was the Divine intent to accomplish this object speedily. The

*Jer. 11:3-9. Pro. 1:24, &c.

people expected to enter in and inherit at
once.   But that generation died in the wilderness, and it is forty years before Israel is
settled in their land.   The cowardice and rebellion of the people hindered.   And while
they could not frustrate divine purposes they
could, and did, delay their fulfillment.   Thus
we have delay, a postponement, such as we
claim in this prophecy of Daniel's, of the
time set for the completion of the divine
purposes.

There are several remarkable prophecies
that present us with this same feature of a
break in their continuity, and singularly
enough they relate to Israel and their acceptance or rejection of their Messiah.   We call
attention to one.   Compare Lu. 4:17-21 and
Is. 61:1, etc.   Why did the Lord close the
book after reading the clause, "To preach
the acceptable year of the Lord?"   There
was but a comma between it and the next,
and they were closely connected by the conjunction *and*.   Why then did he not go on
to proclaim also "the day of vengeance of our
God," and all else that follows?   It is all
one prophetic proclamation.   Clearly, the
answer is, because the carrying out of what
follows was dependent upon the reception on
Israel's part of "the acceptable year of the
Lord," and a recognition of him who pro-

claimed it as their Messiah. In his ministry the Lord is now approaching the close of the 69th week of Daniel's prophecy. The words of Isaiah are the divinely appointed language in which Messiah is to announce his advent, and is to offer himself for acceptance to Israel. Jesus uses these words and thereby appropriates them to himself, and proclaims himself to Israel as their expected Messiah. Will they accept him? He must wait and see. Their future is now in their own hands. It is for them to say whether the remainder of the prophetic proclamation is to go on to its immediate completion or not. Here, as ever, "the awful freedom of the human will was respected by its Maker." They rejected him. The proclamation in its completeness could not be carried out. The day of Israel's redemption must be postponed. It is not forever lost to them. It is still future; but will not be until they are ready to say, "Blessed is he that cometh in the name of the Lord." * This prophecy tells the same story as the one we are considering. The events it announces synchronize with the events that are to follow the close of Daniel's last week, and it presents us with precisely the same hiatus. A rejected Messiah stays the future progress of both prophecies, and

* Matt. 23:39.

when the events of Daniel's last week shall be accomplished, then shall the words of this proclamation be sounded forth again, and this time in all its fullness. The same voice that in Judea eighteen hundred years ago began it, shall now complete it, amid the acclamations of the people, "Blessed is he that cometh in the name of the Lord."

A word in reference to this 70th week, and some of the events that are connected with it as shadowed forth in v. 27.

"*And he shall confirm*," etc. Who is the person here referred to? is an important question. It has called forth many answers. Some consider him the Messiah. This person causes "the sacrifice and oblation to cease," and this, it is said, is what Christ did by the sacrifice of himself. But did he? It was thirty years after his death before Jewish sacrifices were discontinued, and then not because of any influence of the crucified Christ upon the nation, but because of the destruction of their city and temple. And so far as his influence on them is concerned, they would be offering their sacrifices to-day if their temple was still in existence.

Then notice the difference between this covenant and the one Messiah is to make. This person is to make *a* (see marg. and R.

V.) covenant; but Messiah's is *the* covenant.*
This person's covenant is for a week, *i. e.*,
seven years, clearly Daniel's last heptard; but
Messiah's is an 'everlasting covenant.† Then,
again, in the midst of the week this person is
to break his covenant; but Messiah's covenant cannot be broken. The word of the
Lord is sure. His covenant is an everlasting
covenant. Observe, also, that the Lord refers to the events connected with this prophecy as future in his day, ‡ and names the
time of "the end" (v. 14) for their fulfillment. He, therefore, cannot be the person
intended in this 27th verse.

Many historical characters have been named
in this connection, but the only one worthy of
the slightest consideration is Titus, the commanding general when Jerusalem was destroyed. But the destruction announced in
v. 26 is attributed to "*the people* of the prince
that shall come," and not to *the prince* himself. And let it be further noted that the destruction announced in this verse is of the
city and sanctuary, and that it is complete,
fulfilling the threatenings of Lev. 26:14, &c.,
and Deut. 28:15, &c, Whereas, in v. 27 it
is not the city that is to be destroyed, but " *the
Desolator*," who has broken the covenant.

---

* Is. 59:21 cf.; Heb. 8:10.   † Is. 55:3; Jer. 32:40; Ezek.
16:60.   ‡ Matt. 24:15.

(See marg. and R. V.). In these and other respects it will be found that Titus cannot meet the requirements of v. 27.

Who, then, is "*he*"? Observe who are the first agents in this war of desolation that we are told in v. 26 is determined against the holy city, etc. "*The people* (v. 26) of the prince that shall come." In this verse we are dealing with fulfilled prophecy, and we therefore know the people who were the in-instruments of this first destruction. But who is the prince that shall come? It is "*the people*" (the Romans) who shall destroy the city. "The prince" is yet future. The "shall come" belongs to "the prince," not to the Roman people—"the prince that shall come." When? Verse 27 introduces us to him, we think, and tells us something about him. When all the conditions required by the prophecy—a restored nation and a city rebuilt—are in place again, then will the prophecy resume its fulfillment, and then this "prince of the people" (Romans) who destroyed Jerusalem, A. D. 70, shall come. With his coming, the last week of the 70, its interrupted week, will begin to run its course of fulfillment. This prince will then step upon the scene of this world's greatest tragedy. He will make his covenant with Israel, and begin to magnify himself. In the midst of the week he will break his covenant, and will turn his power against Israel, to desolate; but at the determined moment, "wrath shall be poured out upon the desolator." (R. V.)

The "*he*" of v. 27 is, then, we think, "the prince" of v. 26. He is identical with Daniel's "little horn" of chap. 7:7, 8. He springs from that "fourth beast," so dreadful and terrible. All expositors who do not spiritualize the prophecies into airy nothingness, regard this "fourth beast" as the symbol of the Roman Empire, the last consolidated power of Gentile dominion. We further identify this person with "the man of sin," "the son of perdition," spoken of by St. Paul, 2 Thess. 2:3, and the wild beast of Rev. 13:, to whom the dragon gives "his power, and his seat, and great authority."

The following is a summary of the interpretation we have been considering. Seventy weeks (490 years) are determined on Daniel's people. During this period, starting with the restoration, the city is to be rebuilt, reconciliation for sin is to be accomplished, everlasting righteousness brought in, etc., (v. 24).

To this whole period there is given a threefold division. (1) From the decree to restore, etc., (v. 24,) 7 weeks, or 49 years, are determined. (2) From this point to the cutting off of Messiah, 62 weeks, or 434 years.

The combined periods equaling 483 years. (3) One more week remains to complete the whole number (490) of predicted years. But here the onward movement of the prophecy stops. Instead of "everlasting righteousness," etc., we have the announcement of a destroyed city, etc. "War"—Divine chastisement—determined upon Israel because of their rejected Messiah. His cutting off is required of them according to a prior prophecy.* And so long as this controversy lasts "desolations are determined." Israel and Jerusalem are given up to Gentile power to be trodden down. But when "the times of the Gentiles shall be fulfilled," the covenant with Israel will be remembered. They will be restored to their land. City and sanctuary will be rebuilt. Then will the prophecy resume its course of fulfillment, and its last, long suspended week, will begin to run to its completion. On, or about, the opening of this week, a notable personage (v. 27) is to appear, who is to make this week famous. He is the prince of v. 26, of whom it is said—he "shall come." He is of the people who formerly destroyed the city—the Roman. I. e. He will spring from some one of the great powers that in his day represents the fourth beast, or Roman empire.

*Deut. 18:18.

This prince will make "a firm covenant with many" (R. V.), i. e., with Israel. This will be at the begining of the last week. At this time therefore Israel will be restored*. Heretofore—during "many days"—the Gentile has been treading down Israel; now he is to build him up†. He, "the prince," makes a covenant. But he does not keep it. In the midst of the half of the week (R. V.), he begins to exalt himself. As he has done elsewhere, so will he do at Jerusalem. There will possibly be some interference with worship and with religious rites. "And for the overspreading" etc., (see marg.),—"and upon the wing of abominations shall come one that maketh desolate," (R. V.). "Abominations" in the O. T. scriptures often stands for idols‡. "Overshadowing," literally wings (R. V.). It conveys the idea of protection§. The meaning possibly is— for the protection of idols, he shall make it desolate.

But when this half week (3½ years) shall have run its course, the consummation that has been "determined" shall be poured out upon the desolator (R. V.), i. e., upon this prince. He being destroyed, Israel and the world will be ready for the promised bless-

---

*Joel 3:4. Hos. 3:5. †Is. 49: ‡1 Kings 11:5, 7. §Ps. 17:8, 36:7.

ings of v. 24, and there will now be an end of transgressions, etc.

We have dwelt thus fully on this prophecy because it is important in its bearing on our proposed suggestions regarding the Apocalypse. It is the key to our position. If this explanation of Daniel's 70 weeks is right, all that follows seems but a filling up of what he has left unsaid—a filling up of the hiatus caused by the interruption of his prophecy. This interruption began with the cutting off of Messiah, and extends to a point of time yet future. We are living in its times. It has been running on more than eighteen hundred years; how much longer it is yet to run we cannot tell. It is an eventful time, full of history, and God's word is not silent regarding it. Both Testaments speak. Their prophecies foreshadow events down to this last week of Daniel, and through it to "the end." And nowhere are these foreshadowings more remarkable, and more distinct, than in those symbolic representations found in the Revelation of Jesus Christ to the Churches. In these prophecies of both Testaments, four lines of history may be clearly traced, viz.: (1) Concerning Israel, (2) concerning Gentile power and dominion, (3) concerning the Christ, and (4) in the N. T. concerning the Church.

This is the statement we wish to carry
with us to the book of Revelation. This
book we regard as an historic prophecy. Its
utterances and visions have for their subjects
in a special manner these last three histories
as they are influenced by unseen and super-
natural forces, and as they act and re-act one
upon the other. It begins with them somewhat later than the end of Daniel's 69th
week, and it carries them to his last week
and through it, and extends them even beyond the present æon, giving us promises
and glimpses of a new heavens and a new
earth.

As we look at the utterances and visions
of this book, they seem to be a hopelessly
tangled skein. Can they be unravelled?
This is our hope, guided by the light that
other and prior prophecies throw upon the
subject. All have come from the same
source, all must have the same drift. If the
prophetic events of this book synchronize
with the times of Daniel's hiatus, viz., the
interval between his 69th week and his 70th,
and if there are other prophecies of an historical character that evidently belong to this
same period, then it is not unreasonable to
suppose that the prophetic visions of the
Revelation may treat of the same subjects.
If these prior prophecies give us several lines

of history connected with different persons or events, we turn to these last forth-tellings of the spirit of prophecy with the inquiry—do they look in the same direction also? Is it their purpose to unfold to us these same histories, and to cause us to understand more definitely the events to transpire from the time of the suspension of Daniel's prophecy to the resumption of its last week, and on to "the end?"

As a preparation for this proposed study it is important to get before us distinct conceptions of these prophetic histories, and to assure ourselves that they are the subjects of previous prophecies. In this direction we must be very brief. It is impossible even to look at the wealth of O. T. teachings on this subject. Contenting ourselves with references to them in the progress of our study, we pass on to the N. T., and glance at the Lord's prophecy as contained in Matt. 24, and the corresponding chapters of Mark‡ and Luke†.

THE LORD'S PROPHECY.

The time embraced by this prophecy is— "this age" (αἰων). This includes the whole period of the gospel dispensation. It runs from the crucifixion of the Lord and the

---

* Mark 13.   † Luke 21.

organization of his Church, to his coming
again—"the end of the age‡." It thus
synchronizes with the period of Daniel's
hiatus, beginning with the cutting off of
Messiah, and running to and through his
last week.

We find in this prophecy the fourfold history that has been spoken of, beginning, as
we have said, with the time then present
and running on to "the end."

1. *Israel's history*. It is very brief. In
the Revelation it is even more so than here.
There is perhaps, according to our interpretation, not more than one allusion to Israel
throughout that book, and the reason is not
far to find. Israel, though "not cast away,"
has been given up to judicial blindness. In
the exercise of the freedom of the will, they
have rejected their Messiah. As a people
they are suffering the judgments denounced
against them should they be guilty of this
act. So far as their national life is concerned, they are not. They have no history,
save that of the prisoner serving his sentence. And if you would know what that history is, go read the sentence. In Israel's
case we will find it in the latter half of the
26th v. of Daniel's ninth chapter, and still

‡ Matt. 24:3, 13, 14, 30 and 23; 38, 39.

more fully in Lev. 26: Deut. 28:15, &c.; Matt. 23:38, 39; Lu. 21:6, 20–24.

This is not a fancy arrangement to suit the condition of things we are contending for. It is not only in accordance with the positive statements of the divine word as to Israel's present status (see e. g. Hosea 3:4), but it is a repetition of what has actually occurred before. There is a similar instance of such a gap in Israel's history as the one we are now considering, in connection with Jeremiah's prophecy of the Babylonish captivity (Jer. 25:11, and 29:10). The kingdom is interrupted by the taking of Zedekiah to Babylon, and we hear no more of Israel in their nationality from that time on until the expiration of the 70 years. As a nation they cease to have a history until the captivity ends. Israel's sacred history, the history with which the word of God is concerned, is identified with the theocracy. This suspended, Israel's national life is suspended. Their record, as the chosen people, disappears from the divine page. The word of God knows nothing of them save as they are undergoing their sentence. This is Israel's condition now. From the cutting off of Messiah and their scattering, to their restoration, there is, so to speak, an historic parenthesis. The kingdom, in its temporal ascendency and in its spiritual privileges, has been taken from them, and has been given to the Gentile.

In the book of Revelation therefore Israel has no recognition. During the most of the historical period that it covers, Israel has no national life, nor has their history any bearing upon the national life about them. Nor will it, until Daniel's last week begins to run its course. With this week, Israel again take their place among the nations, and after a brief interval of distress, a new and glorious national career opens before them. Hence, we are not to expect mention of Israel in the Revelation, at least not until we are brought to the point where the events of Daniel's last week are recorded.

But when the Lord's prophecy was spoken, Israel still had a place and habitation. We are therefore to expect in his prophecy a history. And we have it. And such a history! Alas, for Israel! Of the temple, there shall not be left one stone upon another that shall not be thrown down. Of the city, it is to be left desolate, and is to be trodden down of the Gentiles. Of the people, there is wrath upon them. They shall fall by the edge of the sword, and shall be led away captive into all nations.

Read, Matt. 23:34-39, and 24:2.

See Luke, 21:6, 20-24.

The prevailing interpretation of this prophecy of the Lord's, is made to center upon the destruction of Jerusalem by Titus. This catastrophy covers the whole ground in the estimation of most expositors. Even the passages that announce the coming of the Lord, find their fulfillment in it. It seems presumptuous to differ from the many learned who agree upon this interpretation. And yet we must presume to differ. There are so many statements of the prophecy that have not met their fulfillment, that we are compelled to dissent from the generally received explanation.

Look at some of them.

1. *The gospel is to be preached in all the world as a witness**. This was not effected at the time of Jerusalem's destruction by Titus; nor has it been accomplished as yet.

2. "*The abomination of desolation,*" *etc.* (v. 15). This was not made to stand in the holy place by the Romans. They were ever scrupulous in respecting Jewish religious feeling. Titus was desirous of saving the temple, and gave command to that effect. The Romans never had access to it. There could therefore have been no abomination set up in its holy place by them, and as the temple has

---

*Matt. 24:14.

ever since been destroyed, the prophecy must yet stay for its fulfillment.

3. *The disturbed state of the nations.* (Vs. 7, 21, 22.) No such universal and tremendous national convulsions took place at, or prior to, the destruction of Jerusalem, and therefore cannot relate to that event, and must be still future.

4. *The general overturning of governments* (v. 29).

5. *The appearing of the Son of Man* (v. 30).

6. *The gathering together of the elect* (v. 31).

In connection with these events take in the following attendant circumstances:

7. *The secrecy of the time when they shall happen* (v. 36).

8. *The suddenness, and therefore, unexpectedness of their happening* (vs. 37-41).

9. *The importance of these events to the Church, and the call to watchfulness* (vs. 24, etc.).

10. *The parables that follow* (chap. 25), and that are a portion of the prophecy, and that can have no adaptation to events that transpired at the time of the fall of Jerusalem.

None of these events, with their conditions, did meet with their fulfillment, as it appears to us, at the time that Jerusalem was destroyed. We are compelled, therefore, in all humility, to dissent from the prevailing interpretation. Israel's history stops with the announcement of the destruction of the city and the scattering of its people. But the prophecy embraces other histories, and in its scope reaches on to "the end."

The destruction by Titus is very distinctly given us in the prophecy, as recorded by Luke, 21: 20 to 24. These statements, let it be observed, are peculiar to Luke. He gives us what the others give, and this much in addition, and we regard this portion of the prophecy as applying exclusively to Israel. It will be noted that (*a*) the period during which this prophecy (in Luke) runs, embraces the days of judicial vengeance, when all the prophetic threatenings against Jerusalem will have their fulfilment (vs. 22, 23): (*b*) The armies are to surround her walls, and the destruction is to be meted out to her (v. 20): (*c*) The Gentile is the Divinely appointed executioner of these chastisements (v. 24). Read in this connection the last half of Daniel's 26th verse (9:), and you may well believe that it is present to the Lord's mind as he utters his prediction. They are marvelously alike in their drift.

Now compare the language of these verses

(Luke 21:) with verses 8 to 13, and 25, 26, and the corresponding verses in Matthew and Mark, and the difference is apparent. Here (*a*) the commotion is world wide. It is nation against nation, etc. (vs. 9, 10). (*b*) There are to be manifestations of false Christs (v. 8). (*c*) There are to be bitter persecutions against the Church (vs. 12, etc.). (*d*) Amid these political overturnings, there are to be natural phenomena (vs. 25, 26) that will appal men, and cause their hearts to fail them for fear of those things that are coming on the earth. There is an universality given to these wars, persecutions and catastrophies, that cannot find their fulfillment in the destruction of Jerusalem by Titus. And there is one other note of difference that must not be overlooked. The end—the bringing to a close of these two prophetic periods is so entirely different, that this alone is sufficient to point out the correctness of our contention. The prophecy (Luke 21:) of verses 20 to 25 (relating as we think exclusively to Jerusalem), ends with "the times of the Gentiles" being "fulfilled." On the other hand, the wars, persecutions and convulsions, of verses 8 to 20, and 25, 26, end with seeing "the Son of Man coming in a cloud, with power and great glory (v. 27).

For these reasons we are constrained to restrict the history of Israel in this prophecy to the portions that have been enumerated, viz.: Luke 21:20 to 25.

2. *The Church.* In the N. T., the Church in its comprehensiveness is presented to us under a two-fold aspect, the outward and visible, and the mystical and invisible. It is the distinction between the professing Christian, who is one outwardly by registration only ; and the professing Christian, who is one inwardly by regeneration. It is the mingling of the elements of the true and of the false. By the first (registration), we have the visible Church, seen and known of all men. By the second (regeneration), there is a number that is known with certainty only to God, and therefore comparatively, unknown and invisible to men. Separate them, and we have the true Church, and the false Church. United and mingling together we have the Church in its comprehensiveness and visibility. Nor is this distinction peculiar to the Church of the New Testament. The O. T. dispensation was a theocracy. All Israel composed the congregation (the visible Church) of Jehovah God. But as a loyal nation and a true Church, its history has been comparatively brief. Long and shameful have been its lapses into idolatry. And yet Israel's God never left himself

without witnesses. There was always a remnant—faithful ones who lifted their voices in protest against Israel's shame. Sometimes indeed they were reduced so low that their testimony was silenced and they were wholly lost sight of. So complete at one time was this hiding, that God had to encourage his desponding servant by assuring him : ''I have left me seven thousand in Israel, all the knees which have not bowed unto Baal, and every mouth which hath not kissed him*.'' They were his faithful ones, his true Church, invisible to the world, but seen and known of him.

In the gospels this distinction comes out in the parable of the tares†. Also when the Lord compares himself to a vine‡ with branches, some fruitful and others not. There are disciples whom he addresses with tender assurances. '' Fear not, little flock, for it is your Father's good pleasure to give you the kingdom.''§ And there are many who in the day of his power will claim him as Lord, and to whom he will declare—''I never knew you''‖. The distinction is constantly forcing itself upon us throughout the epistles. In this historic prophecy of the Lord, it is very marked, as also in the Apocalypse.

---

*1 Kings 19:18. †Matt. 13:24, etc. ‡John 15:1, etc. §Luke 12:32. ‖Matt. 7:21, etc.

In this prophecy the church runs through the same course of time as Israel's history; viz.: From the time then present to the appearing of anti-Christ, and the coming of the Lord. And it is a history of struggle, and persecution, and failure, and patient suffering, and faithful witnessing, and martyrdom, and false prophets, and of many decieved, offended, betrayed, and hatred one of another, and of a great falling away, and of evil servants lording it over their fellows, and saying in their hearts, "My Lord delayeth his coming," and of general unbelief in that event, and unpreparedness for it. Such is the history of the church down to the end of this age— this gospel dispensation, as the Lord pictured it to his disciples.

Matt. 24:4 to 15, and 25:1 to 31, and 10: 16 to 42, and 13:

Mark 13:4 to 14.

Luke 21:8 to 21.

3. *The history of Gentile dominion.* The nondescript beast of Daniel (7:7) had met its fulfillment in the Roman empire. In our Lord's day it was dominating the earth. In this prophecy he announces that it would continue to do so to "the end." Aggrandizement and oppression would still be its ruling passion. It would keep the nations and kingdoms stirred up against each other,

it would persecute the true Church of God,
and it would tread Jerusalem under its feet,
all through its allotted time. The anti-
Christ* is to be its last development. This
will be Daniel's† "prince that shall come"—
the "*He*" of verse 27, and the one who
shall cause "the abomination of desolation"
to stand in the holy place. His career
begins and closes with Daniel's last week.

Matt. 24:15 to 29.

Mark 13:14 to 24.

Luke 21:8 to 13, 25, 26.

4. *The history of the Lord.* This, too,
synchronizes with the other histories. He is
revealed to us in his care over his true Church;
in his coming again; in his gathering together
of his elect; in his judgment on the Church:
and in his destruction of his enemies.

Matt. 24:29 to 32.   25:1-31.

Mark 13:24 to 28.

Luke 21:15, 27, 28.

Such, we think, are the histories outlined
in the Lord's prophecy, and filling up the
hiatus occasioned by the break in Daniel's
prophecy of the 70 weeks.

We are now ready to give our attention to
"the revelation of Jesus Christ, which God
gave unto him to show unto his servants

*Matt. 24:24, 15.   †Dan. 9:26, 27.

things that must shortly come to pass.'' These "things that must shortly come to pass"—are they the histories that the Lord has already outlined to disciples—"his servants,'' on the mount? Is it the history of Israel, and of his Church, and of Gentile dominion, and of his own self, during the interval between Daniel's 69th and 70th week, and on through and to the end of that last week? Such are our convictions. How far there is ground for them can only be determined by an examination of the Book.

THE APOCALYPTIC DRAMA.

We have ventured to speak of this Divine Revelation as a drama. The whole cast of the prophecy is suggestive of this structure. It is broken up into distinct visions with a succession of scenes. A great number of persons are introduced, acting their part and disappearing. There are explanatory agencies and choruses. Nature in all her varying moods is brought in to heighten the effect and to add grandeur, or charm, or terror, as the circumstances may call for. There are the boastings of the self-exalted and defiant, the cruel excesses of the ungodly, the patient suffering of the righteous, and their seeming overthrow. There are battle scenes, and the shout of the victorious, and the cry of the

vanquished. There are thrones and judgments. There is a triumphal procession, and
a marriage, and a marriage feast, and great
rejoicings. The whole book is a succession
of scenic representations.

Should it be suggested that, if it was the
Divine purpose that the book should assume
this form, it would have been so ordered and
arranged; let it be remembered that at the
date of the Revelation, the drama had not assumed the form it now presents. Literary
art in this direction has greatly advanced,
and that, too, only in very recent times.
Modern writers can overcome the difficulties
of arrangement with greater ease and grace
than their predecessors. The drama is now
by means of these improvements another
thing from what it was in the days of the
Greeks and Romans. The breaking up of
parts into acts and scenes, and the introduction of costumes and scenery, have not only
enhanced the attractiveness of the perform-
ance, but they have given to the play itself
coherence, simplicity, and so to speak, self-
explanation. The Author of the scriptures
has never anticipated literary or scientific
progress. He adapts his communications to
the times when, and persons to whom, he
speaks. And so wonderfully comprehensive
have been all these communications, that they

have been found adaptive also for all time and all conditions of men.

This book of the Revelation illustrates this fact. Its structure from beginning to end is dramatic. The divisions which the progress in dramatic art calls for are not perceptible on its face; but they are none the less there. The book is so constructed that it requires but little attention to tell you where these divisions ought to be. They fall into place naturally, and bring out the dramatic feature of the book with great clearness.

This is the object of our present study. We would treat the book as a prophetic-historical drama, and would break up its subjects (histories) into three natural divisions (acts), and these again into such sub-divisions (scenes) as the many-sided incidents of the story seem to necessitate. Comparatively little attention is given to exegesis. It is this structural character of the book, and its probable historical bearings, that will mainly occupy our thoughts. Here and there explanations and proposed interpretations may be necessitated. But in this there is little or no claim to originality. It will be hard to find new thoughts on a subject that has been so much studied and written upon. Doubtless all explanations that may be offered have been suggested before somewhere. It is mainly in the general divisions of the book, and in some of its historical connections, and in the times and dates of some of its events, that there is a departure, so far at least as our information goes, from theories and explanations heretofore put forward.

In studying the Apocalypse we have been led to believe that it synchronizes with the hiatus we have suggested as existing in Daniel's prophecy of the 70 weeks. Between his 69th week and 70th, or last week, there is a break in the onward progress of the prophecy toward its completion. It is a period undefined as to duration, and, by the prophecy itself is passed over in almost complete silence. And yet we know from other sources that it is a period replete with momentous events to the world and to the people of God. It is with these times and histories that we think the Apocalypse deals.

It further synchronizes and harmonizes with the Lord's utterances recorded in Matthew, chapters 10:16-42, and 13: and 24: and 25: It moves along on these same lines of history, treating them with greater fullness, and giving more of detail. Consequently we will expect, if our conjecture is right, to find in in this book (a) a history of the Christian Church in its two-fold aspect, viz: as the Church visible and corrupted, and as the

Church invisible and faithful. (b) We will further expect to find a history of Gentile dominion and its consummation in the Antichrist; and (c) there will also be a history of the Lord Christ. Of Israel, as has been said already*, we are not to expect a history. Nor do we think there is an allusion to them until toward the close of the dispensation, when the events of Daniel's last week begin to run their course. The same principle holds here that was mentioned in connection with Daniel's prophecy. During the greater part of this period, as a nation, Israel is not. The Lord dismissed them from the historic page when he pronounced on them the judgments in Matt. 23:38, 39, and Luke 21:24. And it is not until after these judgments have been executed, and the times of Gentile dominion have been fulfilled—it is not until then that Israel shall once more get possession of their city and country, and as a restored people, Daniel's last week shall begin to run its course. It is at this junction possibly that their existence and their connection with Anti-christ is recognized†. The allusions here to the blasphemies of the Beast in connection with the "tabernacle" may shadow forth the event alluded to by the Lord in Matt. 24:1, 15.

*See page 37.   †Rev. 13:6.

REVELATION 1.

Introduction and Explanation.

The character and scope of the book is distinctly announced to us.   It is a *Revelation*. It was given by God to Jesus Christ, and by him it has been made known to his Church. By a message in the first instance, and then in a succession of symbolic acts or pictures, he presents us with a history of the Church and the world, down to the time of "the end," *i. e.*, down to the time of his coming again.   All this we find in the first chapter. Its opening verses tell us the character of the book, and in v. 19 we have its scope.   The Lord himself seems here to give us the key for its right division and understanding. John is told to write,

(*a*) "*The things which thou hast seen.*" "Seen," or "which thou sawest" (R. V.). The word is here used in a comprehensive sense, and may find its explanation in such statements as John, 19:35, 21:24.   1 John, 1:1, etc.

(*b*) "*The things which are.*"   The things contained in this first chapter and which had just been manifested to him; Jesus revealing himself in his restored glory; Jesus in his relations to his Church—overseeing, inspecting, taking account, approving, disapprov-

ing, warning, counseling, threatening, reward-
ing, punishing; and the Church itself in its
then present condition, a condition unfolded
possibly in the message of the next chapter
to the Ephesian Church.

(c) *And the things which shall come to pass*
(R. V.) *hereafter.*'' These are the things
that are unfolded in the visions that follow,
beginning with the second chapter, and on to
the end.

We must regard this first chapter then as
introductory and explanatory. It tells us
who is the author of the book, and what is
its object. Regarding the book as a dramatic
prophecy we shall break up all that follows
into *Acts*, and these acts again into *Scenes*.
The acts will synchronize, *i. c.*, although relating to different persons and events, they
will run along on parallel lines of time, having a common starting point and a common
terminus. This method is not unusual. It
is unavoidable in historic narrative, whether
sacred or profane. See *e.g.* that of the kings of
Judah and Israel after the separation. If we
are correct in the interpretation of Matt. 24:, we
have in the one prophecy, each of the four
histories, of the Church, of Israel, of the
world, and of the Lord, traversing the same
period of time. And so, through the Apocalypse, we regard the seals, trumpets, etc.,

as different acts, relating to different persons and events, but synchronizing in time.

REVELATION 2: 3:

ACT I.

Subject.—The Church visible.

Time.—From the destruction of Jerusalem to nearly the close of Daniel's last week.

There can be no questioning the object of these chapters. They contain a message to the seven churches from him who walked amid the seven candlesticks, and who gave the command "Write," (V. 1).

"*Seven.*" The number seven plays a conspicuous part in the symbols of this prophecy. It is itself a symbol. We find it all through the scriptures. The subject of numbers has been very carefully studied, and some profess to have fathomed their meaning. The symbolic import of a few seems to be clear. Seven is considered the number of perfection—completeness. It denotes finished work. God rested on that day. His creative work was finished, and ever since, the seventh day by his ordering, is a period of rest—the sign of finished work. It bears this significance in the Mosaic economy—the week, the Sabbatic year, the year of jubilee. Similar is its import throughout this book. The messages to the Churches are brought to completeness in the seventh.

With the Seals and Trumpets, the 6th Seal,
the 6th Trumpet, etc., bring the events they
bear upon to that stage of completeness, that
but one more act is required for the finishing.
The six days brought the creation work to
that point when only one condition was
needed for the completion of the Divine purpose, and the perfection of his work—rest,
enjoyment of what had been accomplished,
and that was the ordering of the seventh day.
So with the successions of Seals and Trumpets.
They are brought down to the sixth, leaving
but one more scene to complete the act, and
consummate the divine purpose.   But that
7th and last act, in each of these instances,
is arrested.   There are other synchronizing
histories that must all be brought down
to the one point of time, and then the catastrophy common to all.   The 7th seal therefore, instead of executing wrath and making
an end, develops into the seven trumpets ;
and the 7th trumpet, for the same reason,
introduces the seven vials ; and these seven
vials in their entirety, represent completeness, especially the 7th, when we have the
outpouring of the wine of the wrath of
Almighty God, even to the last drop—completeness.

When these messages were sent there were
many other churches beside the one men-

tioned. Seven therefore must be used in this connection in its mystical sense of completeness—as standing for all the Churches.

It is possible also that these messages may give us exact representations of the spiritual condition of these several Churches addressed. But we must not confine ourselves to this limitation. The whole character of the messages, and the scope of the book, forbid it. Clearly these are among "the things that shall be hereafter." We must therefore regard these messages as containing a prophetic history of the Church from the time then present to "the end." They are broken up into seven distinct epochs. And what a history it is! Counsels, encouragements, promises, warnings, threatenings, on the one hand ; on the other, some instances of labor, and suffering, and patience, and faithfulness unto death; but a larger and more conspicuous history of love declining, of pervertion of doctrine, of unfaithfulness, and finally, of falling away, and apostasy. It is the same history that we have in Matt. 13:. In those parables but one-fourth of the seed sown springs, and with very varying results. And with this growing seed it is soon discovered that tares are mingled. And as the Church advances to conspicuousness and in-

fluence, the fowls of the air (the world)*
seek it and take possession of it, and
now the woman herself (the Church) having
tasted of the sweets of worldly power, begins
to corrupt herself, and to apostatize from her
Lord. And, last scene of all, the harvest at the
end of the age, the reapers sent forth, and
the gathering of the tares for the burning.
Such is the history of the visible Church as
given us in the gospel by its Divine Head;
and it is the same history that is here presented to us in the Apocalypse by the same
Divine Person. The one is in parable, the
other in the form of a message.

So again, in Matt. 24 (and corresponding
chapters in Mark and Luke), we have first
the struggles and sufferings of the faithful
elements in the Church down to " the time
of the end " (vs. 4-16). In verse 42 to the
end of the chapter, there are intimations of
unfaithful servants who have not watched (v.
43), and of evil servants who believe not in
their Lord's coming, etc., (vs. 48, 49); and
along with these statements are exhortations
to watchfulness that we may escape those
things that are coming upon the earth. And
just so is it in this prophetic history. We have
the same story of loving counsels, of warn-

*v. 19.

ings and threatenings, of falling away and apostasy, until the Lord says: "I will spue thee out of my mouth" (3:16.)—I will utterly reject you. And let it be observed that the messages'stop when the Church reaches that spiritual condition that calls for this threat. The threat is not executed. The message in the prophetic drama brings the Divine intent as far as it can for present purposes, and therefore to completeness. What remains now is execution, and this calls not for words, but for actions. At the appointed time that will come.* But we now call attention to the point at which this 7th message stops, and we beg to emphasize it. It stops with the threat of utter rejection. The reapers are not yet sent forth to gather—out, and to execute sentence upon an apostate Church. The evil is only determined and announced. A little space must yet elapse, and then the Lord will "spue" from him the harlot Church†, and this brings the history of the Church—the Church visible—to perhaps the middle of Daniel's last week. Before the close of this week the sentence will be fully executed.

Of these chapters we make one *Act.* If it is desired to localize the time and events in

*Rev. 17:16, 17.   †17:16, 17.

the Church's history that fulfill the conditions of these several messages, then the *Act* must necessarily be divided into seven *Scenes*. But this is not our purpose. Neither here nor elsewhere in this prophetic history is it our intention to particularize, excepting as it shall be found needful for the understanding and advocacy of the explanation we are endeavoring to establish. Much has been ably written concerning these messages to the seven Churches of Asia. In these writings all who desire to enter more into details will find ample satisfaction. Our purpose is accomplished when we call attention to these messages as a prophetic history of the Church visible, from the time then present, to the close almost of the age. The prophecy stops short with the threatened judgment upon the apostate Church; its execution is yet future.

REVELATION 4:

ACT II.   4: to 8:

Prologue, 4:1-8.

The curtain rises. What a scene is before us! Grand beyond description. Earth never witnessed, no, never dreamed of its like. Its pageants fade into nothingness before it. The first Act was a message—a word communication. Now we are to have a

succession of pictures, with living person-
ages, and stirring incidents.

"*Behold!*" says the Seer.   But first of all
he tells us—"I was in the Spirit."   This is
important.   His being in the Spirit, and his
beholding, are coincident.   We also must be
under the same influences, and in heart must
be occupants of the same place—"Come up
hither," if we would behold and understand.
"Come up hither" is the trumpet call to all
who would read and hear the words of this
prophecy, and who would keep those things
which are written therein.

"*I looked, and behold!*" etc.   We must
then see these things through the eyes of the
Seer.   He must describe them to us.*   We
may therefore regard chapter 4: vs. 1 to 8,
as the prologue to the dramatic history that
follows.   It gives us location.   It introduces
us to a goodly company—the "Dramatis
Personæ," especially as seen in the heavenly
places. *E. g.*, "THE THRONE" in the midst
of heaven, and Him who sits upon it in the
resplendant glory that no man can approach
unto; the Lamb, the Elders, the Living Creatures, the many angels, and along with these
celestial actors we have the scenery and
other accessories that contribute to the better

---

*Ezek. 40:4.

understanding of what is to come, and that
greatly enhances the grandeur of the conception. There are the "four and twenty
seats" (thrones) "round about THE THRONE."
There is the rainbow, and the sea of glass,
and the seven lamps burning, and the thunderings and lightnings, and the crowns of gold,
and the adorations, and prostrations, and
choruses of praise, and the trumpet-voice
with its frequent explanations. This is a
grand pageant. The eye can never weary in
looking, or the ear in listening. But we
must hasten on. This is only the beginning
—the prelude, the solemn and fitting preparation for the awful scenes to follow, and for
the magnificent triumph that is to bring
glory to God, and joy to the universe.

V. 1. "*After this*." (μετα τουτα after these
things) *i. e.*, after receiving these messages
for the Churches. This formula is much
used throughout the book. We have already
met with it in chapter 1:19. We will find
it also in 7:1, 9; 15:5, and elsewhere. In
this verse it occurs twice. In the first instance it clearly denotes the order of time—
after the reception of these messages for the
Churches. At the close of the verse we read
—"I will show the things which must be
hereafter." The Greek is the same. Things
which must come to pass after these things.

Does the formula ($μ.τ.$) in this last instance denote succession of time also? Not necessarily. Lexicographers say that $μετα$, with an accusative, may refer to "succession either of place or time." What is the reference here? Does it in this latter instance refer to an order of time or of place? The context must guide us to a decision. It does in the first instance; let it do so in the second.

The first "after this" is closely linked with the messages to the Churches. It relates to what follows in the order of time after these messages have been received. In connection with the second, let us call to mind that we have been presented with the history of the visible Church. If we are right, it has been brought down to a point when in her self-glorification she is rich, etc. But he who is in the midst of the seven candlesticks says: "Thou . . . knowest not that thou art wretched," etc. "I will spue thee out of my mouth." This is surely a condition of apostacy and pending judgment. Nothing remains but execution— "the end." If it is true that these messages bring the history of the visible Church down to the close of this dispensation, then there will be no time left "after this" for a succession of such scenes as the one presented in the visions that follow. We are therefore com-

pelled by the conditions of the context to regard the last "after these things," as refer-
ring to the order of place—to the order in
which the visions to come will follow each
other.   All the visions cannot be presented
at one and the same moment, any more than
all the incidents of a narrative can be given
at once.   There must be an order of place
for each, although all may belong to the
same order in time.   So with these visions.
From the very necessity of the case they cannot be present at one view.   The observer
could not take them in.   There would be
utter confusion.   There must therefore be
succession.   One vision must follow the
other in an order of place, though all may
be traversing the same period of time.

Of necessity therefore there can be given
the Seer but one picture at a time, and in
receiving them in their order, the most
natural language in which to announce the
ending of one and the beginning of another,
would be that which is here used—"after
this," or "after these things."

Guided then by the requirements of the
context, we regard this last "after these
things," as having reference to an order of
place.   In the order of time the visions that
are to be presented to the Seer synchronize.
Relating to different historical events, they

yet have the same starting point and a common ending. But that the seer may behold correctly and understand, to each vision there is given an order of place, and the coming and going is in an orderly* succession.

"*Come up hither.*" Up to the present, John seems to have been on the earth; he is now called up into the heavens. Throughout he is placed in positions that give him the fullest view of what is taking place. At first he is on earth; then he is called up into the heavens; and at other times he seems to be in mid-heaven occupying a position from which he can command all that is taking place at the same moment, or at least in rapid succession, in both localities.

V. 3. In considering the significance of the Divine appearance, let it be remembered that the two stones "jasper" and "sardine" are the first and last in the breast-plate of the Jewish High Priest.*

"*Rainbow.*" Indicative perhaps that amid coming judgments, the covenant with earth† is not forgotten.‡

V. 5. "*The lightnings, etc.*" take you back to Sinai. They possibly indicate that it is a throne of judgment and fiery indigna-

---

*Ex. 28:17, 20.   †Gen. 9:9, 18.   ‡Ezek. 1:28.

tion; while the rainbow reminds us that covenants of mercy are not forgotten.

"*Seven lamps of fire burning.*" They are explained to us—"Which are the seven Spirits of God." We read concerning them again in the 5th chapter, v. 6.

Fire has always been regarded as the symbol of the Divine Spirit,* the third Person of the adorable Trinity. We have the Father shadowed forth in the ineffable presence on THE THRONE (v. 2), and the eternal Son in the symbol of the Lamb,† and it is appropriate that the Spirit's presence should be signified by these "seven lamps of fire." We must rest satisfied for the present, however, with these statements. Mystery is stamped upon much that we meet with in this book. It is written in letters of light on this symbol — mystery, deep mystery. For a better understanding we must wait until the Spirit himself shall reveal more. Consult, Ex. 37:23, Chron. 4:20, Zach. 4:2.

V. 6. "*A sea of glass,*" etc. Glass and crystal stand for purity, transparency, calmness, permanency. These are attributes of Divine truth. The two symbols, the lamps of fire and the sea, may stand for judgment and truth.‡

---

*Acts 2:1, etc.   †5:6.   ‡Ps. 89:14.

The Elders and the Living Ones. In verses 4 and 6, etc., we are introduced to the 24 Elders and to the four Living Ones. Who are they? These last have been identified with the "the living creatures" of Ezek. 1: and 10:; and also with the seraphims of Isa, 6: and the cherubim of Gen. 3:24. The rendering ("four beasts") of our version is most unfortunate. The Greek word (ζωα) means life. It differs entirely from the word (θηριον) rendered beast (wild beast) in chapter 13:. Opinions are many and divergent as to who or what may be intended by these two representations. The most acceptable until lately, has been the one that regarded them as the impersonations of redeemed humanity, and representations of the executive powers of the Church in the heavenly places. There has always been more or less dissent from this view, on the ground that there were several doxologies relating to the Church, in which the Elders and the Living Ones, either did not take part, or in doing so, did not include themselves. *E. g.*, chapters 7:9, 12, etc.; 15:3, etc., 11:15, etc. The main support for the view that the Redeemed Church was here represented, was found in the doxology in chapter 5:9, etc. "Hast redeemed *us*," etc. But the revisers say that "*us*" is to be omitted. They read—"and didst purchase unto God with thy blood men of every tribe," etc.   This takes away, or at least throws doubt upon, the rendering of the only passage that has sustained the view we are considering.

May not the symbols represent the Principalities, Authorities, Powers, and Dominions, in the heavenlies?   They are enthroned. They encircle THE THRONE.   They are subordinated to Christ,* who is in the midst of "THE THRONE," and of them.†   They wait, they serve, they worship, they praise.   They take an intense interest, an active, willing part, in all that is now transpiring in connection with this drama that we are studying, and they shall joy in the triumph of the Lord.   May they not then be representatives of that "innumerable company of angels,"‡ that belong to Mount Zion, the city of the living God, the heavenly Jerusalem, and that are an important portion of the Dramatis Personæ of our drama?

REVELATION 4:8—11, AND 5:

ACT II, 4: to 8:

SCENE I, 4:8—11, and 5:

LOCATION.—In heaven, and about THE THRONE.

---

*Eph. 1:20, etc.   †Rev. 5:6.   ‡Heb. 12:22.

DRAMATIS PERSONÆ.—He who sits upon THE THRONE. The Lamb; the Living Ones; the Elders.

TIME.—The date of the Apocalypse.

Surpassingly grand is the outburst of praise recorded in these verses (8-11.) The Living Ones begin it with their Trisagion. The four and twenty Elders take it up, and prolong the glorious anthem, amid prostrations and adorations. It is a fit opening for the stupendous drama about to be enacted. This scene is altogether heavenly. The "innumerable company of angels," and the general assembly of the Church of the first-born, are the interested spectators. Every eye is fixed upon THE THRONE. It is the very center of the whole movement. From hence all that is to come to pass, will be overlooked, and ordered, and controlled.

CHAPTER 5.

V. 1. The anthem dies away, and now the onward movement of the drama begins. "In the right hand of Him that sat on THE THRONE," the Seer beholds "a book."

It must have been a roll-book. The Revisers omit the word "side," and read— "written within and on the back."

"*The book.*" This book was sealed with "seven seals." There possibly may have

been seven pieces of parchment, secured one
to the other by as many seals, and all rolled
together, making one roll or book.

"*Sealed.*" The use of the Seal carries
with it several significations in Scripture. *E.
g.* (*a*) It is binding as a witness, as in the
case of contracts.* (*b*) It is a guarantee of
security.† (*c*) It insures secrecy, and that is
its import in this instance. The book was
sealed. Its contents were unknown, and before they could be known, these seals must be
broken.

But who shall break them? Who shall be
counted worthy in that vast assembly to approach THE THRONE, and to take the book
from the hand of him who sits upon it, and
to break the seals, and make known the
eternal counsels of the mind of God? The
question runs through the expectant assembly. The suspense is overwhelming. The
tension is beyond the limits of human endur-
ance. The Seer is prostrated, and gives
way, weeping much, "because no man was
found worthy to open and to read the book;
neither to look thereon" (v. 4). But he is
re-assured and comforted. "One of the Elders
saith unto him, weep not: Behold, the Lion
of the tribe of Juda, the Root of David, hath

---

*Jer. 32:10, &c.   †Matt. 27:66.   Rev. 20:3.

prevailed to open the book, and the seven
seals thereof." The Seer's attention is now
turned to this "Lion" that has been announced. But note that, instead of a
"Lion," there is seen "a Lamb," and the
Lamb had the appearance of one that "had
been slain." It is even so. He is the all-
conquering Lion, because he was first the
sacrificial Lamb, and whether he manifests
himself as the "Lion" or the "Lamb," de-
pends altogether with whom he is dealing.*
To John he appears as a Lamb that had been
slain. To Him has the honor been accorded
to receive the book. He has prevailed—has
overcome, and all power in heaven and earth
has been given unto him. "And He came
and took the book out of the right hand of
Him that sat upon THE "THRONE." At once
the silence is broken, and there is a grand
outburst of praise. Amid prostrations, and
the sound of harps, and the odors of incense,
the Living ones and the Elders lead off the
grand orchestra. Now they address themselves to the Lamb. It is "a new song."
It tells the story of redemption through his
blood. It announces a kingdom purchased
and possessed—a people taken from among
the tribes of men, and who shall reign upon

*Rev. 14:1, 19:7. and 6:16, 19:15, &c. 2 Thess. 1:6, &c.

the earth, and the refrain of their song is
—"Thou art worthy to take the book, and
to open the seals thereof." And the Anthem
grows louder as it rolls on, until "every
creature which is in heaven, and on earth,
and under the earth, and such as are in the sea,
and all that are in them, are heard saying:
Blessing, and honor, and glory, and power,
unto him that sitteth upon THE THRONE,
and unto the Lamb forever and ever." And
so this first scene is brought to its close.

This *Sealed book*, what is its significance?
May we not find its explanation in the first
verse of the Revelation? Contrast these two
portions, and see if there are not features of
strong resemblance. What in that first
verse* is told us in words, seems here to be
unfolded in symbol. In the first instance, a
"Revelation" is announced—something unknown, but to be revealed; in the symbol it
is a book sealed—its contents are yet unknown. In the word-statement, God gives
it, therefore it is in his possession; in the
symbol, the book is in the right hand of
Him who sits upon THE THRONE. In the
word-statement, God gives it to Jesus Christ;
in symbol, the Lamb takes the book out of
the hand of Him who sits upon THE

---

*Rev. 1:1.

THRONE.   In the word-statement, the Lord
Christ shows the Revelation that has been
given him to his servant who is to testify
concerning it; in the symbol, the Lamb pro-
ceeds to break the seals, and summons his
servant to " behold," that he may record
the visions for the instruction of his Church.

This resemblance is very striking. And it can
hardly be presumptuous to answer the question concerning this sealed book by saying,
that it is the same Revelation given to Jesus
Christ, and that it relates to things that
" must shortly come to pass."   It is the
book of the world's and the Church's history,
during the hiatus of Daniel's prophecy; and
it runs from the date of the Apocalypse to
and through his last week.

ACT, II. chp. 4: to 8:
   Scene, 2d. chap. 6:
   Location.   Partly in heaven, and partly on
      earth.
   Subject. Opening of the seals. The course
      of Gentile Dominion with its terrible
      consequences down to the time of the
      end.
   Time.   From the date of the Apocalypse to
      the middle or latter portion of Daniel's
      last week.

The second scene opens. The Lamb is now
the conspicuous personage on the stage.   He

holds the attention of the vast audience. In his hand is the book received from him who sits upon THE THRONE. It is the book of Revelation. It contains "the mystery of God," and "the mystery of iniquity," and the history of the World and the Church down to the time of "the end," and the Church of Christ, and the Mighty intelligences of the Universe desire to look into these things, and are waiting with intense eagerness.

He opens one of the seven seals. Immediately, in tones of thunder, one of the Living Creatures cried—"Come." The R. V. omits, "and see." The command is therefore issued to the ordained symbol. And straightway there passes before the Seer's vision "a white horse." "He that sat on him had a bow, and a crown was given unto him, and he went forth conquering and to conquer."

"*A white horse.*" And what of this horse and his rider? It is of course a symbol. But whom does it represent, and what does it signify? Surely not Christ. The fact that the riders here and in chp. 19:, are both on white horses and wear crowns, is not ground sufficient to establish identity between them. The similarity is easily accounted for. The horse personifies strength. The white horse indicates victory, and triumph; and a crown is always the emblem of royalty and kingship. The Lord Christ is not the only one who lays claim to these prerogatives in this world. There is "a prince of this world," who, pointing to its kingdoms, dared to say even to the Christ: 'All these things will *I* give thee, if thou wilt fall down and worship me." He claims this world as his. He wears its crowns,* and transfers them to whom he pleases.† And his mastery over it, and impress upon it, is unmistakably manifest everywhere. The white horse and the crown, and all that they symbolize, are not therefore in this world and at this time, the exclusive right of Him who opens the seals. In this symbol an usurper sits upon the white horse, and guides him on his conquering career. For so is it "given unto him (V. 2)."

Observe also other considerations that will not suffer us to recognize the Lord Christ in this symbol.

(*a*) This rider is nameless. Wherever the Lord Christ is brought before us, there is no attempt at disguise. Whether as the Lion, or the Lamb, or the King of Kings, there is no mistaking him. Attending multitudes, the glorified Church—the all-beauteous Bride,

---

*Rev. 12:3.   †13:2.

the hallelujahs, the crowns at his feet, the Armies of heaven following him,—always is he proclaimed the Christ of God. He is no longer nameless. He cannot be obscured. God has highly exalted him. God—He who sits upon THE THRONE, has given Him a name which is above every name. Any allusion to him must cause the knee to bend, and the tongue to confess, and the anthem of praise to ascend. No nameless horseman then can symbolize Him. When His time comes, and he mounts his horse, his names shall be blazoned on vesture and thigh, and the tramp of his conquering legions shall stir the heart of the Universe.

(*b*) This horseman comes with "a bow." But this is not Christ's weapon. When he rides forth, he bears a sword. The bow is the instrument for the discharge of arrows. The arrow, the dart—"fiery darts," these in the New Testament are Satan's weapons. The Lord Christ has no identification with him and with his weapons.

(*c*) This horseman, as a royal conqueror must be identified with the times of this present dispensation. But these attributes of kingship and conquest do not appertain to Christ at this present time. This is the dispensation of the Spirit. The gospel is being preached as a witness. A people are being gathered out of all kindreds and nations for his name. But He, the risen Jesus, is in the heavens. They have received him and* must retain him, until the times of the restitution of all things. In His providential dispensation he, of course, over-rules all things; but his special work is now " within the veil." It is here that His official relations to His Church are being exercised. He is Prophet, Priest, Sacrifice, Intercessor. Take the scene we are considering as illustrative. He is before us as the Lamb Slain—the sacrifice. Where is he? In heaven, before THE THRONE. And what is he doing? Exercising his Prophetic office—opening the sealed book that he may " show to his servants things that must shortly come to pass."

He is then exercising his offices in the heavens, and is not on earth. He is not on his own throne. " Now we see not all things put under him." He is on his Father's throne, not his own. His kingly office is as yet in abeyance, and must continue so until he takes unto himself his " great power," then shall he reign. We cannot therefore recognize the Lord Christ in the symbol of this conquering horseman.

(*d*) And yet further we would call atten-

---

*Acts 3:21.

tion to the attendants of this horseman—
war, famine, death. These are not the
attendants of the Prince of Peace. He is
never presented to us with such surroundings. True his presence brings a sword
upon the earth. But *He* does not draw it.
On the contrary his command is—"Put up
again thy sword into his place." His mission is peace on earth, good will toward men,
and even when he does take unto him his
"great power," and comes to reign, there
will indeed be judgment quick and sharp,
but his attendants are the armies of heaven
clothed in white, and riding on white horses;
and in the day of his sovereignty, swords
will be beaten into plow-shares, and spears
into pruning-hooks: nation shall not lift up
sword against nation, neither shall they
learn war any more.

We therefore cannot recognize Christ in
this symbol. To us it in no way speaks of
him. Of whom or of what then does it
speak?

We suggest that it stands for Gentile
Dominion. The existence and character of
this power has been brought to our notice
before in prophetic symbol. The metallic
image of Daniel represents it in its totality.*

---

*2:31, &c.

This image is a perfect man from head to feet, and so it continues until "the stone" smites it. There is, however, well defined divisions in the image. In the interpretation we are told that they denote four successive empires, and yet the unity of the image is not broken. No matter what different metals or substances may enter into its composition, yet, from its head to its feet, the one idea (Gentile Dominion) is embodied.

These different parts of the image are in Daniel's vision symbolized by four Beasts. He describes the fourth Beast as "dreadful and terrible, and strong exceedingly; and it had great iron teeth, it devoured and brake in pieces, and stamped the residue with the feet of it."*

It is this terrible nondescript Beast that we are now most interested in. It is the last of the four Beasts, and it therefore represents the last period of Gentile Dominion, the period in which we are now living. It answers to the legs of iron, and the feet, part of iron and part of clay, of the image. Most expositors see a connection between this symbol and the Roman Empire. In the Lord's day the government by military tribunes had passed away, and Rome had

*7:7.

assumed the purple, and was stretching forth its arms in Conquest. At the time of this Apocalyptic vision, it had reached the zenith of its power, and war, famine and death, marked the advance of its legions.

According to our scheme of interpretation, the history of this Gentile Dominion must be found in this book, and here we think we have it. This symbol of the white horse and its rider, and his attendant horsemen, tells the story with all the distinctness of the other symbols that relate to this subject, and that have preceded it. It synchronizes with the legs and feet of Nebuchadnezzar's image, and with the nondescript Beast of Daniel's vision. It portrays this power as it then was, as it since has been, and as it will continue to be to "the end." The color of the horse (white) denotes triumph. The crown given the rider is sovereignty, his weapon is death dealing, and his mission is conquest. This is the Divine ordering for this power down to "the end." It was to be an instrument in his hand who ruleth in the armies of heaven and upon earth, to "overturn, overturn, overturn, . . . until he come whose right it is to reign."* To Nebuchadnezzar, the first acknowledged

---

*Ezek. 21:27.

head of this power, it was said: "The God of heaven hath given thee a kingdom . . . and wheresoever the children of men dwell, . . . hath he given into thine hand, and hath made thee ruler over them all."* Of Daniel's fourth Beast it is said: "It devoured and brake in pieces, and stamped the residue with the feet of it."† And here it is again. A symbol armed for destructiveness, commissioned for conquest, and attended by war, famine, pestilence and death. What can be more terrible? And the picture is true to the life. Read history and see these awful outlines filled up. And even now, though some years of peace have intervened, yet the governments that continue to represent this Gentile Dominion, are armed to the teeth. They are crushing out the life of the people asking for bread, and they are watching their opportunity to spring at each other for conquest. Not only is Jerusalem to be trodden down by it, until the times of the Gentiles be come, but all the peoples of the earth. It "shall devour the whole earth, and shall tread it down, and break it in pieces." ‡

V. 3. The second Seal is opened, and here, as in the other instances,§ the command "come", is to the appointed symbols. These

---

*2:37, 38.　†7:7.　‡7:23.　§Vs. 1, 5, 7.

horsemen follow each other in rapid succesion. We do not regard them as independent and separate symbols, each shadowing forth a different person or event, but as parts of one symbol—the White horse and his rider with his attendants. The White horse leads, these follow. The four unite to make the one symbol. As the different metallic substances unite in the making up of the one image of Nebuchadnezzar's dream; so here, the four horsemen unite to give us a complete symbol. The first horseman by himself is incomplete. Associate him with the others and we have a finished picture that tells its own story. As a symbol it takes its place unmistakably beside those found in Daniel, and we are impressed with the fact that it represents Gentile Dominion down to "the end" with its misrule, with its greed, persecutions of the Church of God, and oppression and massacre of the peoples of the earth.

The two pictures that follow vs. 9-17 present us with the result of this domination. And they are (*a*) a persecuted and slaughtered Church; and (*b*) a devastated and terror stricken earth.

V. 9. The scene is now in heaven, but is closely linked with the one that has just preceded it. The opening of this Seal brings to our notice for the first time the real

Church of God—the true, the faithful ones. They are the Souls that are with Jesus. They are resting, waiting, expecting. They have passed through their fight of afflictions. They have been faithful even unto death, and they are now witnessing against the mis-rule and God-hating spirit of this Gentile power.

They are seen under the Altar. On the Altar is the place for the offering; beside it is the position of the priestly offerer; but "under" it—at its base, is here designated as the place of rest—"rest yet for a little sea-son", is the answer given them. It may also carry with it the idea of safety. In all countries and religions the Altar was the place of sanctuary. The man whose life was forfeited sought refuge at the Altar. If there was safety anywhere, it was there.* And these souls were in the place of safety, be-yond the reach of Satanic hate, and the World's persecution. But though safe, they are not dissociated from earth. They are in the fullest sympathy with their brethren who are yet bearing the heat and burden of the day, and together with us, they are anticipat-ing "the end"—the day of vengeance of our God.†

---

*Ex. 21:14. 1 Kings 2:28, etc. †Luke 18:7.

V. 12, etc. The sixth Seal is broken. The picture now presented is the second evidence of the misrule of this Gentile domination. The Most High entrusted it with power, and it has abused it. In the fifth Seal was heard the cry of the Church against it. Here we have a picture of the condition into which it has brought the earth through its cruelty, ambition, and God-defying spirit.

Sun, Moon, and Stars, stand for persons of distinction. Note Joseph's dream, Gen. 37:9, etc. Consult also, Rev. 1:20, 9:1, Num. 24:17, and Matt. 2:2, Dan. 8:10.

Earthquakes and natural disturbances signify political and social upheavals and horrors.* While it is not improbable that when the events called for by this seal shall be transpiring there may be great natural disturbances, as at the time of the Lord's crucifixion, yet we are disposed to regard this and similar discriptions throughout the book, as figurative, announcing social, rather than natural convulsions.

The closing of this scene is tragic and awful to the last degree. The "White Horse" and his attendants have done their work effectively. In addition to wasting and desolating the earth, Gentile Dominion has also blas-

---

*Is. 2:10, etc., 13:9 etc.,34: 2 Peter, 3:6, etc.

phemed the God of heaven, and defied his
sovereignty, and, as we shall learn elsewhere
in the book, has compelled the nations to do
the same. And now the time of reckoning
has come. The hand-writing is on the Wall.
The characters — "*Mene, Mene, Tekel,
Upharsen*", are blazoned in letters of light.
Even a scoffing world can no longer doubt.

The events of this seal bring us down in
all probability to the beginning of Daniel's
70th week, and consequently to the uprising
of the Anti-Christ. It must even continue
well into the week—to a point of time when
a rebellious, God-defying world begins to
realize that there is an all-conquering power,
that his terrors are abroad, and that the day
of his wrath has come. It is the day of consternation foretold by the Lord in Luke 21:
25, 26. "Upon earth distress of nations,
with perplexity; the sea and the waves (the
enraged peoples) roaring: men's hearts failing them for fear, and for looking after those
things which are coming on the earth: for
the powers of heaven shall be shaken." See
also Isa. 2:12, &c.

But here let it be carefully noted as
important to our scheme of interpretation,
that in the events taking place under this
seal, verse 27 of Luke has no place. "And
there (in the midst of this expectancy and

consternation) shall they see the son of man coming in a cloud, with power and great glory.'' Events under this seal stop short of this consummation. Doubtless it is expectancy of this coming, that gives occasion for the World's consternation. But events under this seal stop short of it. It is this fact that we want especially to emphasize. This sixth seal brings the world's history—the history of Gentile Dominion, down to a point of time just prior to the Lord's Advent, and there it stops—there it leaves it. There is more to come, but this seal is not to tell it, nor is this history to be further pursued for the present. This second scene of Act II, closes, leaving Gentile Dominion still in existence, but in a state of terror and fearful expectation. This, it will be remembered, was precisely the condition in which the visible—the false and apostate Church, was left at the close of Act I. Its prophetic history of chapters 2: and 3: closed, leaving it still in existence, a self-righteous, rejected Church, with threatened judgments awaiting the hour of execution. The two histories in the two Acts traverse the same period of time. The one tells the story of the Church down to the moment of its rejection; the other brings the history of Gentile Dominion to a similar moment, when it too has been judged, and its heart is failing it for fear. In both instances we naturally look for the onward movement of the history, and for the execution of the threatened judgment. But not so. Other histories, and strange events must be narrated, and must be brought down to this same point of time, before "the end" will be announced. The judgments and awards are alike for an appointed time, therefore must the history of all be first brought down to that day and hour, before the Drama can unfold the judgments in their execution, and the honors in their bestowment.

REVELATION 7:

ACT, II. 4: TO 8:

Scene.—3d. chap. 7:

Location.—Partly in heaven, partly on earth.

Dramatis Personæ.—Angels. The Sealed. The Elders. The Lamb.

Time.—The entire period of O. and N. Testament dispensations down to the translation.

This third scene presents us with the history of the hidden Church. We have already had in Act I, a history of the Church visible—the Church as it is seen by the world, and that indentifies itself with the world, and that eventually apostatizes. The history of Gentile Dominion, with its cruelties and godlessness, was the subject of the next scene. Now there is given us what to the world is a hidden history. It relates to the Church invisible—the sealed ones. We have already called attention* to the fact that the Church is made up of these two elements. In the history of the visible Church (Act I) —the Church of the world and of the Apostasy, we read of those who have labored, who have not fainted, and have suffered tribulation and poverty, and have not denied the faith, and have been faithful even unto death. What of these? Where are they? They cannot be identified with those who left their first love, who consented to the doctrine of Balaam, who associated themselves with the woman Jezebel, and who have joined the synagogue of Satan? Certainly not. They have a separate history, and this scene tells us all about them.

No Seal is here opened. They (the Seals) belong exclusively to Gentile Dominion, and the results of its mis-rule. This picture-history may be regarded as an explanation and expansion of the fifth seal. There we were shown the souls—the victims of Gentile per-

---

*p. 44, &c.

secutions, sheltered beneath the Altar.　This scene tells us more about them.　It is the history of the true Church, the Church unrecognized by the world, and unknown to it; but sealed of God, and therefore known to him, and kept by his power, and that will at last be gathered before THE THRONE, and before the Lamb.　(V. 9.)

V. 1.　The scene opens with a beautiful conception and illustration of Christ's headship over all things for his Church.*　Four Angels standing on the four corners of the earth, hold the four winds of the earth, that they should not blow on the earth, nor on the sea, nor on any tree.　The earth is doomed.†　"The winds,"—the forces of nature and the passions of evil intelligences, are ready at any moment to break loose and destroy.‡ But God has his purposes.　He holds them in check.　His Church is still in the world. All have not been gathered yet, and until they are, the restraining Angels must stand to their posts.

V. 2.　Another angel is now seen ascending from the east—"the sun-rising" (R. V.). His course is from the East to the West.　In his hand is the Seal of the Living God, with which he is to seal the servants of his God.

---

*Eph. 1:20, etc.　†2 Peter 3:5, etc.　‡Jer. 51:16.

Farther on* we read of an Angel flying in the midst of heaven with the everlasting gospel to preach unto them that dwell on the earth. This is the fact revealed here. It is a symbol of the Church commissioned to go into all the world and preach the gospel. This preaching began in Jerusalem.† Its course has been steadily westward. Its mission is to proclaim the grace of God, and to take out from among the Gentiles a people for his name.‡ "He that believeth and is baptized shall be saved." But before this calling out and sealing process begins, the messenger Angel gives charge to those holding the four winds, to keep them in check. "Hurt not the earth, etc., till we have sealed the servants of our God in their foreheads." (V. 3.).

And to-day we can look with John upon this striking picture. To those who have eyes to see and ears to hear, it is as distinctly set forth in the heavens as when the seer beheld it. The restraining Angels are still at their posts. The apostle Paul announces that the mystery of iniquity was working in his day—that it only awaited the removal of a restraining power, and then will he be revealed, the lawless one, whom the Lord Jesus will consume, etc.‖ The existing World

---

* 14:6.   †Acts 1:8.   ‡Acts 15:14.   ‖2 Thes. 2:7, etc.

power—the Beast so dreadful and terrible, the lawless one, whose coming is after the working of Satan with all power and signs and lying wonders*—this world power is restrained, until the sealing is finished and the number of the elect completed. "All things continue as they were from the beginning of the creation", † is ever the taunt of unbelieving scoffers. They dream not that destructive forces are ready to burst upon them, restrained only by Divine command. The world continues as it is for the sake of the Church, until the servants of God shall be sealed.

The gospel message proposes a compact. If accepted, it involves agreement and action between contracting parties—"believe and be baptized, and thou shalt be saved." God and the believing soul entering into Covenant. This sealing is then the sign of these Covenant relations. It signifies identification, ownership, security. (*a*) It is the Lord knowing them that are his;‡ (*b*) it is giving this knowledge to them that are his, sealing them with the Holy Spirit of promise;‖ and (*c*) it is his people desiring this knowledge—"Set me as a seal upon thine heart", etc.§ And this sealing is "in their foreheads".¶ All men must be able to know them at once. By

---

*Dan. 7:7, 2 Thes. 2:7, etc., Rev. 13. †2 Peter 3, 4. ‡2 Tim. 2:19. ‖Eph. 1:13, etc. §Cant. 8:6. ¶Ezek. 9:4, etc.

the confession of the mouth, and by the manner of living, it must be manifest to all that
they have been with Jesus, and that they are
witnessing for him.

V. 4. In this fourth verse the result of
this sealing is given. The messenger Angel
has therefore accomplished his mission. The
number of the elect is completed, and the
time of "the end" is reached. This is
further confirmed by the fact that the earth-
picture here closes, and we are introduced to
a heavenly one (V. 9). Behold the multitude of the sealed ones gathered on the
Mount Sion.

This determines also for us the time occupied by the vision. It extends from the
first sending forth of the gospel on its mission of calling and sealing down to the
translation.* This event takes place just
prior to the Lord's appearing. Its period
synchronizes then exactly with the other histories we have been considering. It is the interval between Daniel's 69th and 70th week,
and runs on to perhaps the middle of that
week.

" *Israel.*" This numbering is said to be
among " the tribes of the children of Israel."
Our vision relates immediately to gospel

---

*1 Cor. 15:50, etc., 1 Thes. 4:13, etc.

times. Israel as a nation are not.* They
are in blindness and banishment. This is
the dispensation when God is taking out a people for his name among the Gentiles.† This
gathered people are declared to be Abraham's
seed, and heirs to the promises.‡ So that
we are authorized in interpreting the term·
"Israel" in its largest spiritual conception.

These gathered people belong to both dispensations. Under the Theocracy there was
a "holy seed"—sealed ones. So hidden
away were they at times that one of the most
distinguished of the prophets was not aware
of their existence. But God knew them.
These are their successors—their brethren.
What if those of the present dispensation
were once alienated, and enemies in mind by
wicked works? Yet now hath he reconciled
them in the body of his flesh through death,
to present them holy and unblamable and
unreproveable in his sight.‖ They are
all one in Christ Jesus. Both Jew and
Gentile are comprehended. Verse nine requires this. Here is the aggregate of
this sealing—"A great multitude, which no
man could number." Who are they? They
are "of all nations, and kindreds, and people,
and tongues." This is exactly what the

*See p. 37, &c. †Acts 15:14. ‡Gal. 3:29; Rom. 2:29.
‖Col. 1:21, 22.

apostle James declares to be the present mission of the gospel;* and it is in connection
with this fact also that the Living Ones
count Him, who had received the book,
worthy to be praised and honored—"for
thou wast slain, and didst purchase unto God
with thy blood men of every tribe, and tongue,
and people, and nation."† "Israel"
stands then for the Redeemed of Christ.
Nor, as we take them in the aggregate, must
we limit them to the called of this dispensation. While we regard the historic limits
of this vision to be the gospel period, yet
when we come to consider these sealed ones
as a great multitude, and as the same company that we read of in chapter 14, we must
recognize the saints of the Old Testament
dispensation as well as those of the New.
We must include that faithful company
recorded in Hebrews 11:, and "of whom the
world was not worthy." The sealed ones in
their completed numbers are the Lamb's
Bride—the Redeemed of all generations and
of all nationalities.

"*An hundred and forty and four thousand.*"
So in regard to this numbering. The very
genius of the book we are studying requires
that this number, as well as the term "Israel"

---

*Acts 15:14. †Rev. 5:9.

shall be taken figuratively. The aggregate of this sealing is, we are told, "a multitude, which no man could number." Then it is impossible to give the exact figures. There must be some "x" that shall stand as the sign of the unknown quantity, and we have it in the number designated. In symbolic numbers, twelve is supposed to be the number of the heavenly, the perfected Church. There are twelve patriarchs, twelve tribes, twelve apostles, twelve thrones, twelve stars,* twelve gates.† One hundred and forty-four thousand is the multiple of twelve. This number must then be regarded as a representative one. It stands for the whole multitude of the Redeemed throughout all the ages down to "the end."

V. 9. "After this," *i. e.*, after the sealing has been finished. The first part of the scene was an earth-picture. It calls our attention to four angels standing on the four corners of the earth, and holding in restraint the four winds of earth that they should not destroy. It shows us the messenger Angel moving from the sunrising, and sealing the servants of God, and it gives us the result of this finished work. Now we have another picture. It is in the heavens. The sealing

---

*Rev. 12:1. †Rev. 21:14, 16.

is finished, and the translation, described in
I. Cor. 15:50, etc., and again in I. Thess.
4:13, etc., has taken place.   This multitude
is composed of those who during the ages
past have slept in Jesus, together with those
who at the time of his appearing were yet
in the flesh, and were caught up to meet him
in his coming.

Nor must it be supposed that in this
picture we have an overlapping of the time
limits of the other histories.   Not at all.
These two events, the sealing and translation,
and the conquest mission of the " white
horse," move along on the same parallels of
time.   They reach their terminus at or about
the same period.   The history of the Apostate
Church was brought down to a point where
sentence awaited execution.   So in the history of Gentile Dominion, the nations are
affrighted, and men are realizing that the
great day of wrath is at hand.   And in this
scene, the history of the faithful Church is
brought down to the time of its removal
from the earth.   This wrath cannot be
poured out while any of the sealed ones are
here.   The command to the angels is—hold
the winds until the sealing is finished.
These sealed ones must be beyond their
hurt.   And this is what our last picture presents.   It shows us the redeemed Church on

Mount Sion, safe with its Lord. There is nothing now between the world and the on-rushing winds of destruction. The Angels but wait the command. And so the histories of the Apostate Church, of the godless world power, and of the faithful Church, are brought down to the same awful moment in time—judgment threatened, and certain, and all ready to be executed on an evil world and an Apostate Church; but the true Church is safe. The five virgins whose lamps were burning, have entered in with the Bridegroom. The door is shut. While *without*, men's hearts are failing them for fear of impending judgments, in this heaven-picture we are presented with the scene *within* the closed doors—the Church safe, and rejoicing, and adoring Him that sitteth on *The Throne*. This scene has correspondence and close connection with chapters 12:5, and 14:1 &c.

What follows from v. 13 to end of chapter, does not properly belong to the picture. It is explanatory. We shall meet with such interruptions or additions often in the course of the drama. It is a filling up of the pictures. Telling us in word-pictures what cannot be so well expressed by symbol. In the present instance it is one of the Elders explaining to the wondering Seer the personnel of this worshiping rejoicing throng.

They are not the multitudinous Angel host.
Neither are they of the order of the Living
Ones, nor of the Elders, nor yet come they
from the ranks of Cherubim or Seraphim; but
from earth, out of great tribulation, and
have washed their robes and made them
white in the blood of the Lamb. What
follows is anticipative, and tells of the
honors and glories of the Redeemed Church,
and transports us to the scenes connected
with chapters 21: and 22:

But the historic pictures are not yet all
completed. Others are to be presented, and
to be brought down to this same moment of
fearful waiting for of judgment, before the
actual outpouring of the vials of wrath can
be described. We now pass on to Act III,
and its several scenes.

REVELATION, 8: 9:

ACT III.   8: to 11: 1–15.

Scene 1st.—Chapters 8: to 9:

Location.—Partly in the heavens, and partly on the earth.

Dramatis Personæ.—The Lamb, Angels, Trumpeters, Men.

Time.—From Apocalyptic date to the beginning or middle of Daniel's last week.

The Seer is still in the heavenly places. He is before THE THRONE, and in the presence of the Lamb, and the great multitude of attending angels.

There are seven seals. The 6th at its close showed us Gentile dominion ripe for judgment and expecting it. There was also given us a glimpse of "the Church of the First Born" in heaven. They have not only escaped those things that are coming upon the earth, but by their absence the barrier that hindered these threatened judgments has been removed. We should expect, therefore, all things being now ready, that the opening of the 7th and last seal would usher in the climax of the tragedy—the threatened judgment executed. But it does not. The seal is broken, and instead of the winds being let loose, and the storm of Divine wrath sweeping in its fierceness over

the earth, we read—"there was silence in
heaven about the space of half an hour"
(v. 1).

Is it the silence of rest? Is it to give the
Seer's mind time to adjust itself for the new
series of events that is to be brought before
it? Is it carrying out our idea of the
dramatic structure of the book, the dropping
of the curtain to allow the shifting of the
scenes preparatory to a new Act? We are
disposed to think so.

The seventh seal then, instead of bringing
the drama to a close, contains and unfolds
the prophetic symbols of a new *Act* with its
succession of *Scenes.*   There are yet other
histories connected with this "mystery of
iniquity" that must be disclosed. The
Book taken from the hand of Him who sits
upon THE THRONE contains "the whole
course of the world's history." The seals,
the trumpets, the vials, are parts of this
whole. The seals contain the trumpets, the
7th or last, develops them. So from the
trumpets come the vials. They are successive acts presenting us with parallel histories.
In Act I, it was the Church corrupting
itself.*   In Act II it was Gentile dominion in its pride, and greed, and cruelty.

---

*Rev. 2:3: Matt. 13: 33-36.

Here (Act III), it is the history of Satanic power under spiritual guises assailing the Church and the World. In the former case, it was the material world-forces working out, through Satanic energy, their awful consequences upon the nations. In the symbols now to be presented, we have, energized by the same power, a history of the spiritual world-forces within and without the Church. The spiritual elements predominating throughout these scenes lead to such an interpretation, if they do not necessitate it. E. g. The Altar, the censer, the incense, the fire from the Altar, the prayers of the saints. These are all spiritual in their relations. So also in regard to the ultimate results upon men, as presented by the 6th trumpet. They become worshippers of devils, and of idols of gold and silver, neither repent they of their murders, of their sorceries, fornications, or thefts. *

Without this representation, the Apocalypse as a prophetic history would be incomplete. This spiritual world-force working its evil, is as conspicuous in its destructiveness, as the material world-force in its oppressions. From the very beginning it has opposed itself to the word of Jehovah God. You can trace it from Jannes and Jambres, who withstood Moses,†

---

*(9:20, 21.). †2 Tim. 3:8.

down to the close of the O. T. dispensation.
And from the very outset of the present it has
sought, and to the end will it continue to
seek, the overthrow of the gospel of the glory
of Jesus.   In the Acts of the Apostles, that
tell us of the first planting of the Church, we
read of Judaizing teachers.   The Epistles
warn against Gnostic heresies, and in this
book of the Apocalypse, we read of the Nico-
laitans, and of the doctrine of Balaam, and
of Jezebel the prophetess and seducer, and of
the synagogue of Satan.   Passing on to Ecclesiastical history, we find its pages occupied
with controversies concerning Arianism, Pe-
lagianism, Socinianism, and spiritual world
forces without end.   And with the years, the
number and intensity of these assaults upon
the word of God and the gospel of Jesus, have
multiplied.   These are the spiritual world-
forces within the Church.   And from without, from the world itself, they have been no
less numerous and persistent in their assaults.
From the day that Elymas, the sorcerer, withstood Paul* to the present, the succession has
been unbroken.   It counts in its ranks such
names as Celsus, Julian, Porphery, Mahom-
med, Gibbon, Voltaire, and such like, all
children of the devil, enemies of all righteous-

---

*Acts, 13:10.

ness, perverters of the right ways of the Lord.
And to-day the world is full of them. Wheresoever their origin, and whatsoever their tend-
encies, they all have a common center of
unity—hatred of Jesus, contempt for his cross,
and rejection of his Kingship. In the present
day these spiritual forces are multiplying and
exercising a wide-spread influence upon the
minds of men both within and without the
Church. Their tendency is to undermine the
authority of Scripture as the word of the
Lord, to dethrone God from his universe, and
to make men return to the worship of de-
mons, and to all immorality. The material
world-forces presented to us under the seals,
culminate in the Beast of the sea, of Chapter 13:1, etc. These spiritual forces find their
culmination in the Beast of the earth—the
false-prophet of the same chapter, V. 11,
etc.

Vs. 1–6. Possibly it is during the continuance of this silence that the seer has the
opportunity of taking in his new surroundings. THE THRONE is still there. The
grand tableau of chapter 4 is a permanency.
It is ever present to the seer. He is ever in
the midst of its glories. It is not only a representation of Divine Majesty, but it is THE
THRONE itself which is from everlasting to
everlasting. And God is on it. He has de-

serted neither his universe, nor his earth. Not a sparrow falls to the ground without his permission. There have been times when indeed it has seemed otherwise, and it will be so again. But THE THRONE is still there. God reigns. By his secret providences he rules and restains. Upon the raging madness of ungodliness, he lays his hand, and says: "Hitherto shalt thou come, but no further; and here shall thy proud waves be stayed."* This is one of the facts that the Revelation is intended to teach, and to impress, on the minds of God's people. The world will not recognize it.† But to those who are "in the spirit", THE THRONE and he who sits upon it, are always visible.

In this new vision therefore THE THRONE is still present to the seer. And now standing conspicuously by it are seven Angels. To them seven trumpets are given. The Angel beside the Altar, and the burning incense, and the fire from the Altar poured on the earth, with its direful results, these are all preparatory, and as we have suggested, explanatory.

V. 6. And now the first Angel sounds. Are there historic facts in the direction suggested that correspond to the symbols of these

---

*Job, 38:11.   †Is. 10:5, etc.

six trumpeters? It is not our purpose to attempt an answer to this question. Many ex-
positions have been made, and those who
would go more into this matter, will not be
disappointed for lack of material.

Chap. 9:1. We call attention to this 5th
trumpet, because, (*a*) it is ushered in by a
special announcement. An Angel (8:13) is
heard "flying through the midst of heaven,
saying with a loud voice, Woe, Woe, Woe,
to the inhabitants of the earth, by reason of
the other voices of the trumpets of the three
Angels, which are yet to sound." This cry
is doubtless intended for the Church. There
will be a portion of it in the days of these
trumpeters that will have ears to hear. For
them the warning is intended. Knowledge
has increased, and with it the power for evil
as well as for good. There will therefore be
an increased intensity in spiritual wickedness,
and in the afflictions that flow from it. And
(*b*) it is furthermore worthy of remark, that
there is great unanimity among expositors in
recognizing in this symbol the rise and
career of the Mahommedan power.

V. 12. At this point there is an interruption to the onward movement of the drama.
An explanation must be given. This was
common, and a necessity in the Greek plays.
By the introduction of scenery and dress,

and other improvements in the dramatic art we are able in our dramatic representations to dispense with these interruptions. The voice is both explanatory, and a note of warning and preparation. It announces that one woe is past, and that two more are to follow.

V. 13. The 6th Angel sounds, and immediately a voice from the altar bids the trumpeter (v. 14) "loose the four angels which are bound in the great river Euphrates." The Euphrates in that day was the border line between the civilized and the barbarous—between culture and savagery. Interpreting the command as the language of symbol, we may regard the "Euphrates" as the boundary between the material and immaterial—between the land where there is God, and Christ, and hope, and the realms of outer-darkness. And the character of these Angels to be loosed must be determined by the results of their loosing, and these are awful in the extreme. The announcing voice may well give warning of coming woe. They are none other than Satanic agencies— spirits of evil, that in the working out of "the mystery of iniquity," He who sits upon THE THRONE, suffers to visit the earth, and to influence and energize those who will not obey the truth.

These Angels are not to be confounded with those mentioned in chapter 7:1. The position and mission of those Angels of the winds are entirely different. They are holy ones, and throughout these prophetic times they are still at their posts holding in reserve the agencies of Divine judgments, while these emissaries of evil are pursuing their mission. In chapter 16:13, we read of an occurrence not unlike the one we are considering. Here the spirits are three. They come out of the mouth (the device and counsel) of the dragon and his materialistic agencies. They are not identical, and yet they probably stand in close relations. These four Angels of darkness are the sowers of the tares—the scatterers of the seeds of endless heresies throughout Christendom, and are thus preparing the way for these unclean spirits.

V. 15. The R. V. translates—"Which had been prepared for the hour, and day, and month," &c. From this improved reading, the inference is that the reference is to the arrival of an appointed time. The fullness of the time had now come, even to the very hour, when these Angels were to be loosed and sent on their errand. And what an awful one it is—"for to slay the third part of men." We must take this, as we are doing the other

portions of the vision, in a spiritual sense.
It is a spiritual slaughter that is intended.
These emissaries of Satan are probably those
"seducing spirits" of whose appearance in
the latter times, the Divine spirit warns the
Church. * They are to teach "doctrines of
devils, and speaking lies in hypocrisy."   As a
consequence, there is to be "a falling
away."† Nominal Christendom will make
shipwreck of its faith. Men will cease to
"endure sound doctrine."   After their own
carnal and materialistic desires shall they
heap to themselves teachers, having itching
ears; and they shall turn away their ears
from the truth, and shall be turned unto
fables.‡ Are we in the beginning of these
times? Have these Angels of darkness been
let loose upon Christendom? And in the
higher-criticism, in agnosticism, and univer-
salism, and unitarianism, and conditional
immortality theories, in Theosophism, and
Positivism, and scepticism that is everywhere
cropping up in a thousand forms,—are these
"the army of the horsemen" that these
Angels of the Euphrates are to lead forth on
the earth? Surely "perilous times" must
result from their presence. For from these
teachings men will "become lovers of their

---

*1 Tim. 4:1. †2 Thess. 2:3. ‡2 Tim. 4:3, 4.

own selves, covetous, boasters, proud, blasphemous, . . . lovers of pleasure more
than lovers of God; having the form of godliness, but denying the power thereof,"* By
these "doctrines of devils" shall the third
of men be slain.

In executing their mission these Angels
send forth an immense body of horsemen,
Attention has been called to the fact that the
horses in this symbol, rather than the riders,
are the conspicuous agencies, and the questions
asked are these, "Is the intimation intended
that these riders (heretics) are, in many
respects, not so bad as their horses (death-
breathing heresies)? Or is it suggested that
the horses (the heresies) ordinarily run away
with them (the heretics); that they speedily
lose control over the movements originated
by themselves? Possibly both thoughts are
intimated."†

V. 19. "*Their power*"—the power of
this legion of horsemen (heresies), "is in
their mouth, and in their tails." The mouth
is the organ of speech. It is by speech, and
its adjunct, the printing press, that they
disseminate their "lies." "And their tails
were like serpents, and had heads"—their
doctrines were Satanic. They were inspired

---

*2 Tim. 3:1, &c. †Lange's Com. on Rev., p. 200.

by that "old serpent, the devil, which de-
ceiveth the whole world."*   They related to
the earth, and the worship of devils, and the
idolatry of gold and silver, &c.†

In chapter 12:4, it is the Dragon's tail that
"drew the third part of the stars of heaven,
and did cast them to the earth." Both
symbols, we think, relate to the same apostasy,
and represent the wisdom of the world made
all powerful by Satanic energy and cunning.

The results produced by these spiritual
world-forces under the 6th trumpet, ‡ are
precisely analagous to those produced under
the 6th seal ‖ by the material world-forces.
In the former symbol (the 6th seal), the
scene closes with the political world-forces
(Gentile dominion) in upheaval and consternation because of expectant § evil.   And so it
is left.   The final catastrophy is, to the Seer,
still pending.   Meanwhile his attention is
called to other considerations.   So here we
have precisely the same conditions.   There
are seven trumpets.   Six describe the spiritual apostasy of Christendom.   Of Christendom, not of the Apostate Church.   Keep this
distinction clear.   It is the utter abandon-
ment of Christianity for "the doctrines of

*Rev. 12:9.   †V. 20.   ‡Vs. 20,21.   ‖6:15-17.   §Lu. 21
25, 26.

devils," through the agencies of spiritual
world-forces ("damnable heresies"), that
these trumpet symbols treat of. The sixth
trumpet, like the sixth seal, brings its
apostacy to the full, with its terrible consequences realized; but Christendom still defiant and impenitent, and persevering in its
wicked courses. And just at this point the
curtain drops. The history of this apostacy,
as in the case of the defiant world-power in
the sixth seal, is for the present suspended.
The next scene opens, and in it our attention
is fascinated by new objects and histories.
There is yet another trumpet, the seventh
and last. But the Seer is not ready for it.
When it sounds, it announces development
—a progressive movement along the whole
line of the prophetic history.

According to our scheme of interpretation
the apostate Church in chapters 2: and 3:,
the God defying world-power under the 6th
seal, the Redeemed Church under the same
seal, and apostate Christendom under the 6th
trumpet, are brought down to the same
moment of time. The Redeemed Church is
removed that it may escape those things that
are coming on the earth, the others are
awaiting results with anxious forebodings.
In prophetic time this will bring us somewhere from the beginning to the middle of

Daniel's last week—the week of the anti-christ.

The seventh trumpet will call us to an onward movement in the prophetic history. But the Seer is not yet ready for it. This "second woe" trumpet has not entirely told its story. The Church—the witnessing, faithful Church, has a deep and painful interest in it, and this seventh trumpet must not sound until these things are set forth so far as Divine purposes will allow.

REVELATION 10.

ACT III.   8: to 11: 1-15.
Scene 2d—Chaps. 10:11: 1-15.
Location.—Mostly on earth.
Dramatis Personæ.—Angels, the two Witnesses, the Beast, the Seer, dwellers upon the earth.
Time.—Synchronizing mostly with the period of the 6th seal, and 6th trumpet.

This scene is located principally on the earth. It concerns mostly the witnessing Church. "Ye are my witnesses,"* is the Lord's parting announcement to his disciples. And from that day to this the world has never been without witnesses, and never will be,

*Acts 1:8.

even to "the end." It is concerning the persecutions, sufferings, death, revival, and translation of these witnesses, that we are now to hear. The events recorded, especially in the 11th chapter, belong to "the latter days." They synchronize with events connected with the 6th seal and the 6th trumpet, and they bring us possibly to Daniel's last week.

Chap. 10: The position of the Seer seems to have changed. At first* he was summoned into the heavenlies, a location which he has continued to occupy to the present time. Now, however, he is seeing and speaking, as from the earth. †

The symbols of this scene are difficult of explanation—"things hard to be understood." We must be satisfied in regarding them as events yet future, and connected with the Witnessing Church—the "little flock," the Church that is faithful and true. We have had recognition of this Church before (7:) as the Sealed ones—the separated from the Apostate Church, the protected, and at last, by translation, the Church delivered from impending earth judgments.

V. 1. John sees "another mighty Angel come down from heaven, clothed with a cloud;

---

*Chap. 4. †10:1, 8, 9.

and a rainbow upon his head; and his face was as it were the sun, and his feet as pillars of fire.'' This Angel, by most expositors, is identified with Christ. But the similarity of this appearance with those of Rev. 1:13, etc., Dan, 7:13, is not a certain guide to such a conclusion, for we have a somewhat similar description of one who evidently is not the Lord Christ. Dan. 10:5, etc., cf. V. 13, etc.

V. 2. In his hand is "*a little book*". There are four books brought to our notice in the Apocalypse: The sealed book in the hand of him who sat upon THE THRONE ; * this little book in the hand of the Angel ; † the books of general record; ‡ the book of life. || This book contrasted with the others is called "little," because perhaps it contained the record of only the Church, with a glimpse of the glory that should follow. It was therefore small in size, and could quickly be read through.

V. 4. "*Seven thunders . . . uttered their voices.*" We listen to the thunder with an instinctive consciousness that it is God's voice, that he is speaking from the heavens. Here again we have the number seven denoting completeness—perfection. In the symbol we recognize a Divine revelation. God makes

* 5:1. † 10:2. ‡ 20:12. || 20:12, 15, 21:27.

known to his servant some things that must shortly come to pass. But when the Seer would write in compliance with previous instructions,* he is commanded: "seal up those things which the seven thunders uttered, and write them not." Here, as in Chap. 5, sealing stands for locking up—concealing. † These utterances remain therefore among the "hidden things." Many have surmized that they relate to the Reformation of the 15th and 16th centuries. But when the words are sealed, who can tell?

V. 5. The Angel still occupies the same position that he did when the seer first beheld him.‡ And what a grand conception is here given us!‖ This mighty Angel of such majestic proportions, and glorious appearance,§ is seen standing on sea and land—significant perhaps of world-power and culture beneath his feet ready to be trodden upon; with right hand uplifted to heaven; with leonine voice that penetrates to the uttermost bounds of the creation, and that asseverates "by him that liveth forever and ever" the verity of the proclamation about to be announced; with all intelligences in the universe attentive, expectant, and awaiting the things to be revealed; this is the unfolding of a picture

---

*1:19.   †Is. 29:11, 12.   ‡V.2.   ‖Dan.12:7.   §V. 2.

surpassingly grand. We surely need to be "in the spirit" to grasp it in its splendor and magnitude. "There shall be time no longer; but in the days of the voice of the seventh Angel, when he is about to sound, then is finished the mystery of God, according to the good tidings which he declared to his servants the prophets" (R. V.).

Wonderful and welcome announcement. It is the consummation long and devoutly wished for. Angels have ever desired to look into these things;* disciples asked—"when?"† The souls beneath the Altar cried—"how long!"‡ and the whole creation together with the struggling Church, have ever been groaning within themselves—"waiting."|| Welcome indeed is the announcement of the mighty Angel to those who have "ears to hear."

V. 6. "*There shall be time no longer*"— time shall no longer be, i. e., the appointed delay is at an end. That "little season" announced to the inquirers beneath the Altar§ has now reached its limit.¶ It was needed for the sealing of the entire number of "the elect,"** and it was symbolized by the four restraining Angels.††

---

*1 Peter 1:12. †Matt. 24:3. ‡Rev. 6:10, &c. ||Rom. 8:22, &c. §6:11. ¶Ezek. 12:27,28. **7. ††7:1, 3.

V. 7. This consummation is now near at hand. It only waits the voice of the seventh Angel. When he shall begin to sound, it will be the signal to the waiting universe that "the mystery of God" is finished. The wisdom of God has been working out the problem of evil in the presence of his intelligences. Our earth has been the arena —the central location, perhaps, where these puzzling questions have been presented. The presence of disloyalty and discord; the unequal struggle between the good and the evil; the apparent triumph of the powers of darkness; the heir sent to the vineyard and cast out and killed; Satan still allowed in the heavens; his work upon the earth unhindered; the Lord Christ not upon his throne, and his people still struggling and suffering because of their witness for him; these are some of the mysteries of God. The purposes long hidden away from his creatures, are now to be unfolded. The problem of evil has been solved, and when the seventh Angel sounds, great voices in heaven will be heard saying: "The kingdom of this world has become the kingdom of our Lord, and of his Christ; and he shall reign forever and ever."* (R. V.)

---

*V. 15.

V. 9. The Seer is commanded to take the little book from the hand of the Angel, and to eat it. To eat, as the mind eats, by reception and apprehension. It is an open book, and therefore easily read and understood. The effect of this eating is at first sweetness to the mouth, but afterward bitterness to the inward parts. There was a charming fascination experienced as the unfoldings of the prophecy revealed to him the good things that were to come;* but his after reflections, when he came to consider the apostasies, blasphemies, and terrible judgments, and the much tribulation of the Church,—these things cause him great bitterness—heaviness of soul.

V. 11. "*Thou must prophesy*, &c." To prophesy is used in both Testaments not only as fore-telling, but also in the sense of forth-telling, announcing, teaching. It is probably in this larger sense that it is used here. The explanation given by some expositors is, that at the Reformation John's teachings would be revived in the Church, and thus, though dead, he would yet be prophesying.

Chap. 11: All expositors concur in regarding the symbols of this chapter as difficult

---

*Dan. 7:28, 8:27, 10: 1-4, 16, 17, 21.

beyond any others. Alford says: "No solution at all approaching to a satisfactory one has ever yet been given of any one of these points."

V. 1. A measuring reed or rod, is given the Seer, and he is required to "measure the temple of God, and the Altar, and them that worship therein."* The measuring must be taken in a figurative sense.

"*The Temple.*" According to the theory on which we are basing our structural arrangement of this Book, at this stage of the prophecy, we are at, or about, the beginning of Daniel's last week. If so, Israel must at this time be restored,† and their city must be in their possession.

To what then is the reference here? Is it to Israel after the flesh, and to Jerusalem, and to the semblance of a temple service that they may have in that day? Or, are we to regard the imagery of this vision as symbolic, and treat it as we have done that of all the others? Israel, we have said, will be restored at this time. But they will be restored to their land in unbelief.‡ It is not probable that there will be any attempt, or even disposition, to erect a temple. Syna-

---

*Ezek. 40:3, &c.; 42:15, &c. Rev. 21.15, &c 2 Kings 21:13. †See p. 20, &c., and 32, &c. ‡Jer. 31:31, &c. Ezek. 20: 40-45. 39:27, 28. Joel 2. Zach. 12:10. &c., 13:

gogue worship will be the most that they
will aspire to. And it is not until Israel shall
behold their Priest-King, and shall welcome
him with—"Blessed is he that cometh in
the name of the Lord,"—it is not until then,
that this will be the holy city, and that the
glories of the temple service will be restored. *
The events mentioned in verse eighth, and
which are connected with the city "where
our Lord was crucified," clearly indicate the
fact of a restored Israel at this time, and the
attitude they will then assume toward the
witnesses for Jesus.

Mount Moriah and its temple is undoubtedly the picture here presented to the Seer.
He beholds it in all its glories. But temple,
and altar, and outer court, are not. They
were things of the past. The things therefore seen in the vision must be symbolic,
and their relation must be to the Church,
and to the God-defying world-power! If we
except the statements of the eighth verse,
there is nothing in the symbols of this
chapter that can fit in with Israel after the
flesh. Then, as now, judging from verse
eighth, they will be antagonistic to the
witnesses for Jesus. If we will look for their
history at this special point of time as given

---

*Ezek 40: &c., &c.

us in other Scriptures, we will find that it is entirely different from events as here narrated. The Church—the true Church, and the World, are clearly the subjects of this prophecy. As evidence of this, note the fact, that as in the symbol (6:) of the downward career of the material world-force, there is attached a prophecy of the condition of the true Church (7:); so to the history of the spiritual world-force (9:), there is appended in this chapter (11: 1-15) we are now considering, a history of precisely similar import —a body of faithful ones, under the symbol of two witnesses, witnessing, suffering, and eventually translated. We must therefore regard the two histories as one, and relating to the same subject, viz.: The true Church.

We interpret then the temple and its altar-court with its worshipers, as representing the Church. The Church visible and invisible, and its worshipers of all kinds, the true and the false. The Seer is to measure them by some spiritual standard, and is to see whether they come up to the requirements. And this is perfectly in harmony with what we are elsewhere told. We are nearing "the end." The World is ripe for judgment. The time has come, and it must have its beginning "at the house of God."* And here

---

*1 Pet. 4:17. Ezek. 9:6.

it is.   Perhaps it is at this time and to this
assembly, that the warning cry of chap. 18:4,
is being raised—"Come out of her my
people."

V. 2.   " The court that is without," i. e.
The world.   It is not to be measured.   It belongs to the Gentiles, to Gentile dominion.
It is still under the sway of this Godless
power.   No need of measuring it.   It has
been judged already.   See this judgment in
chaps. 6: and 9:, and we shall learn more of
it in connection with events that follow the
voice of the 7th trumpet.

This "Court," the World, is given into
the hand of Gentile dominion—the great and
dreadful Beast, and "the holy city" even, the
true Church, "shall they tread under foot."

This prophecy is to be carefully distinguished from that in Luke 21:24.   There the
prophecy is concerning Jerusalem, the Jerusalem of our Lord's day.   There are no
references in that prophecy to temple, altar,
and courts, nor is the characteristic "holy"
applied to it.   There it is the material city and
its inhabitants that are to be given up to Gentile dominion.   The temple and altar are not
excepted.   The whole city, and all its be-
longings, are given over, and that too for a
prolonged and indefinite period—"until the
times of the Gentiles be fulfilled."   But here

the language is clearly symbolical. It ap-
pertains to places and conditions that have
ceased to be, and must therefore be taken in
a spiritual sense.

If the temple, and altar, and them that
worship there, are symbolic and figurative,
then consistency requires that the reference
to " the holy city " should also be so regarded.
If the temple, &c., stands for the true priest-
hood who alone have a right to enter and to
minister within its precincts; then " the
holy city " must stand for the holy people
who alone have a right to inhabit it.

This " holy city "—the faithful and true
Church, shall Gentile power tread under
foot. This it has always done, as will be
seen in chaps. 6: and 9:. But just at this
special time, probably the beginning of
Daniel's last week, there seems to be given
it larger license, as the symbolic language
and prophetic statements that follow, indicate.

The time here designated (v. 2) for this
treading under foot becomes, after this, an
important factor in our considerations and
interpretations. We shall now continue to
meet with it, and to find it linked with most
of the important histories down to "the end."

The period here designated is " forty and
two months" $= 3\frac{1}{2}$ years. In the next verse

(3) we are told that the "two witnesses shall
prophesy a thousand two hundred and three
score days"=3½ years. The "Woman
clothed with the sun" is to be in the wilderness (12: 6 and 14) "a time, and times, and
half a time (1260 days, v. 6)=3½ years, and
power is given the Beast (13:5) for the same
period. Now observe that this note of time
is conspicuous also in Daniel's prophecies.
We have it in the form—"a time, and times,
and the dividing of time," i. e., one year,
two years, and half a year=3½ years, (7:25,
12:7, cf. Rev. 12:6, and 14). In Daniel's
prophecy concerning the last week of his
seventy, his week is to be halved by important events. During the first half, a covenant is to be made between restored Israel
and " the Prince " of the people who
destroyed the city after the cutting off of
Messiah. But in the midst of the week
(9:27), it is to be broken. Now, three and
a half (3½), the number of our consideration,
is the half of seven, and let it be further
noted, that Daniel's use of that number is
always in connection with "the Prince,"
the covenant breaker, the blasphemer and
oppressor, the anti-christ. In meeting with
this number (3½ years) again in these, as
we believe, closing prophetic records of the
world's history, we are irresistibly led to the

inquiry—Are the two prophetic eras the same? Are we in Daniel's last week? Everything tends to strengthen that impression. And we must not omit calling attention to the fact that in Daniel's prophecy* we have a similar scene to the one we have been considering in Rev. 10:6. Daniel† sees the man clothed in linen, standing on the water of the river, with hands lifted to heaven, taking a similar oath, that the desolations concerning the holy people (Israel), should not be prolonged beyond "a time, times, and half a time." In both instances the Angel's oath precedes this specified time, and limits the events they speak of to this so well defined period. Are these two periods then one and the same? We think so. We think that they refer to Daniel's last week. In the Angel's oath in Daniel's prophecy, however, the three and a half (3½) years have reference to the last half of his week, which will be the period of Israel's great tribulation, growing out of their connection with this prince, and the broken covenant; while in this oath in the Revelation, the reference is evidently to the first half of this same week. During this first half Israel and "the Prince" will be in agreement, and will

---

*12:7. †12:7.

be of one mind in their treatment of "the Witnesses."*

If our explanation is correct, then the treading down of "the holy city," the true Church—the Church of the sealed ones, is the subject of this prophecy, and is continued on to verse fifteen (15); and its time is the first half of Daniel's last week.

Recall the history of the sealed ones (7:). We brought it down to the translation, which we supposed would be about the middle of Daniel's last week. Under different symbols and names, we have here† we think, a repetition of the same history. The first was a history of the true Church in its relations to the material world-forces; this second is a history of the same Church in connection with spiritual world-forces. Both histories run parallel with each other, and are identical. Three and a half (3½) years before the translation (the first half of Daniel's week), the power to tread down "the holy city," will be granted the anti-christ, the Beast that ascendeth out of the bottomless pit (V. 7). He will at this time be coming to the front. For his own crafty purposes he will have made his covenant with restored Israel, and will be promoting the interests

*Rev. 11:8.   †11:1-15.

of the material Jerusalem; but the true
Church will be under his heel. The witnesses for Jesus throughout the World, will
be the objects of his hate and persecution,
and it will continue for three and a half
years, down to the translation. This event
(the translation) will be immediately followed
by the voice of the 7th Angel (V. 15), and
this is the date (the middle of Daniel's last
week) to which we have brought down all
the histories.

V. 3. "*My two witnesses.*" As witnessing can only be for Jesus,* it would seem
that it must be Jesus speaking here. But
that does not necessarily follow. At the
opening of the Book, we are told that Jesus
sent and signified the things to be made
known by his Angel (1:1). He is here probably speaking by his Angel, who impersonates him. An instance of this occurs in
chap. 22: 6-10. The Angel emphatically
impersonates the Lord—"Behold, *I* come
quickly;" and in the next breath we find
him refusing the offered adoration, and
announcing himself as a "fellow-servant."
See also v. 16.

A peculiarity of these two witnesses is,
that "they shall prophesy . . . clothed

---

*20:4.

in sackcloth." Sackcloth is a penitential dress. It must indicate the distress of spirit that will weigh down these witnesses in these days of their testimony. Fortunately it will be short. We are now possibly approaching the times to which the Lord referred when he said: "Except those days should be shortened, there would no flesh be saved; but for the elect's sake those days shall be shortened."* The allotted time, for these sackcloth witnesses, is 1260 days, or 3½ years.

And who are these witnesses? In V. 4, we are told that they "are the two olive trees, and the two candlesticks standing before the God of the whole earth."† From the language used they seem to be persons, and the powers attributed to them,‡ seem to make this view imperative. Hence many have supposed that two of the old prophets would be sent on this mission. John has been named as one of them·‖

If, however, it is admissible to explain the language figuratively, we would suggest that the *two Testaments*, the Old and the New, are the two olive trees. The olive tree is the source of the oil that supplied the Sanctuary lights. The two Testaments are for us

*Matt. 24:22. †Zach. 4:3, 11, &c. ‡Vs. 5 and 6.
‖John 21:23,

the source of Divine truth. This truth is witnessed-to in the world by God's faithful people through (1) preaching, and (2) the printed page—the two candlesticks, or lampstands. But it is the body of true believers—the true Church of all generations, that always have been the witnesses, and that in this coming time, will in a special manner bear their testimony, clothed in sackcloth.

Vs. 5 and 6. We must let these verses pass without suggestions. They give personality to the two witnesses. We must class them among "things hard to be understood." It is as yet a sealed prophecy. But when the time comes, it will speak, and will not lie.

V. 7. "*The Beast* . . . *of the bottomless pit*" is to be the instrument in the slaying (silencing) of these witnesses. Who is he?

In Daniel's vision,* the four winds of the heavens "strive upon the great sea." The sea symbolizes peoples, &c.,† and a sea disturbed by winds suggests social and political upheavals. His four Beasts, in their ordered successions, were to arise out of the social disorders and political convulsions of the na-

---

*7:2.   †Rev. 17:15.

tions.   John in his vision, saw the same
thing.   His Beast, the last of Daniel's four,
comes up also out of the sea.   His "ten
horns" identify him with Daniel's last
Beast.*   Out from among these horns, in
Daniel's description, there comes up another
"little horn".   In John's vision, it is a
head.   He sees it "as it were wounded to
death, and his deadly wound was healed".†
In common with all the others, he too comes
up out of the stormy sea; and we are further
told, that he was energized by the dragon.‡
Thus his origin is not only from the sea, but
from "the bottomless pit" from whence he
received power, and derives his spirit of
hatred against the people of God.   "The
Beast out of the bottomless pit" is then the
"little horn" of Daniel's vision.‖   He is
also "the Prince" of his last week,§
and he is the one who in our Book is de-
scribed¶ as the head wounded to death, and
afterwards healed.   In a word, he is the
Anti-christ, of whom Paul tells us in 2
Thess. 2:6, &c.   This is the power that is
allowed to make war against these witnesses,
"and shall overcome them, and kill them"
(v. 7).

   V. 8.   "*Their dead bodies.*"   The voice

---

   *7:7, 8.   †13:3.   ‡Vs. 2, 4, &c.   ‖7:7, 8.   §9:26, 27.
¶13:3.

of the witnessing Church is silenced.   They
are to the world as dead.   Perhaps a decree,
like that during the French Revolution, will
be issued by the Beast from the bottomless
pit.   "The book of the Lord" will be proclaimed fabulous.   Its doctrines will be stig-
matized as dangerous to social order, and
those who hold them will be required to de-
sist from teaching them.   And so the witnesses for Jesus and his Gospel of grace will
be killed.   This is not only probable, but
facts yet to be brought to our notice, make
the issuing of such an edict certain.   In
commanding the worship of himself, the
Beast must prohibit all other worship.*

The dead bodies of these witnesses are to
lie "in the streets of the great city, which
spiritually is called Sodom and Egypt, where
also their Lord was crucified".   That the
reference here is to the city of Jerusalem
seems very clear.   According to our theory
the events now under consideration—the witnessing, the killing of the witnesses, are connected with the first half of Daniel's last
week.   According to the interpretation given
elsewhere,† Israel will at this time be restored, and will be in close alliance and
friendship with the Anti-christ, "the Beast

---

*13:4, 14, &c.   †P. 20, &c., and 32, &c.

out of the bottomless pit." This decree therefore may have been issued from Jerusalem, and so, the death blow having been struck in that city, the dead bodies may be said, in a figure, to be seen there also.

Vs. 9, 10. "*They that dwell upon the earth shall rejoice over them.*" Not only will Israel be in sympathy with the aspirations of the Beast, and with this his decree; but the earth-Beast also,* and the harlot woman,† and all peoples of the earth. The witnessing concerning judgment to come, and a returning Christ, and redemption through the blood, has become both distasteful and hateful. The wisdom of the world despises this word of the Lord, and pronounces it false. The power of the world is disturbed by it, as was Herod by the questioning of the wise men.‡ And the harlot woman has long ago hidden away this word, and forbidden its use, and misrepresented its doctrines. The world is therefore weary of it. The testimony of the witnesses is a continual source of alarm. It keeps it in a state of unrest. It is tormented by it. The world rejoices therefore because their voice has been silenced.

Vs. 11, 12. But this rejoicing is not long.

---

*13:11, &c.   †17:   ‡Matt. 2:

The dead bodies are suffered to lie exposed and dishonored only for three days and a half. The 1260 days (v. 3) are taken literally. We must so regard these three days and a half. They are literal days.

That our suggestion regarding the "two witnesses" may be perfectly clear, we will re-state it. They are the succession of true believers, who in all ages have testified for God. They may derive their designation—"two witnesses," from the fact that the two scriptures of the Old and New Testament are now the sources from which they draw their doctrine and inspiration. By means of the speaking voice and the printed page, the true Church holds these scriptures forth as the word of life* to an ignorant or unbelieving world. This is the position assigned to the Church by her Lord from the first.† And the true Church has ever been a witnessing Church, basing its testimony on—"Thus saith the Lord". Its appeal in both dispensations has been to the scriptures—"to the law and the testimony".‡

Now this rejoicing on account of the killing (suppression) of the Word of the Lord, and of them who bear it, by (as we have sug-

---

*Phil. 2:16. †Acts 1:8. ‡Is. 8:20, John 5:39, Matt. 24:14. See Peter's Ser. Acts 2:14, &c., and Stephen's Argument, Acts 7:

gested) the infidel powers of the world, is of
short duration.   Three and a half days after
the issuing of the decree against the scriptures, there is a revival of the dead witnesses.
And how is this effected?   "The spirit of
life (v. 11) from God entered into them, and
they stood upon their feet; and great fear fell
upon them which saw them."

In 1 Cor. 15:51, 52, and in 1 Thess. 4:13
&c., the Apostle Paul teaches that at the return of the Lord, his believing and waiting
ones will be caught up to meet Him in his
coming.   The same fact seems to be taught
by the Lord in his parable of the ten virgins
(Matt. 25:).   Have we a reference here to
this event?

The world is ripe for judgment.   It
has now perpetrated its last crowning act of
iniquity.   It has not only refused to hear
sound doctrine, but has denied the Lord who
bought it.   It has decreed God's word out of
existence, and so far as the will power goes,
has banished Him from His throne, and it is
now rejoicing in its supposed triumph.   What
more that is impious can it do?   Judgment
will now be surely swift.   But the faithful
ones—the sealed ones, must not be involved
in it.   "Watch, and pray always," was the
teaching of their Lord, "that ye may be
counted worthy to escape those things that

shall come to pass.''* And these waiting ones, witnesses for their coming Lord, will surely be removed, as Lot from Sodom, before the bursting of the fiery storm. And so it is. In one place Paul tells us—"the trumpet shall sound;''† in another, he says,—"the Lord himself shall descend from heaven with a shout, with the voice of the arch-angel, and with the trump of God; ‡ and here we are told—"they (the witnesses) heard a great voice from heaven,(v. 12). And this voice, this "trump of God," gives no uncertain sound. To these suffering witnesses it is the long expected summons—"*Come up hither.* And they ascended up to heaven in a cloud," (v. 12). In a moment, in the twinkling of an eye, they were changed, and were with the Lord. If we would know what would follow this ascension, read Chapter 7:9, to end, and Chapter 14:1, &c. These are scenes in the heavens. What of the earth? "Their enemies beheld them" in their ascending. Was it to them an ocular demonstration? Perhaps not. It was sudden, noiseless, only those summoned heard the call. Two were in the field, the one was taken, and the other left. Two were grinding, the one was taken, the other left.‖ Their enemies mis-

---

*Lu. 21:36. †1 Cor. 15:52. ‡1 Thess. 4:16. ‖Matt. 24:40,41.

sed them. They learned of their sudden disappearance. But whither? And as this inquiry for the missing ones would circle round the earth with the rising sun, the only response to this world-wide cry of alarm would be from the word of God—they have been caught up to meet their coming Lord—they have escaped those things that are coming on the earth. Yes, the word of the Lord still lives. Human decrees cannot annul it. Heaven and earth shall pass away, but not one jot or tittle of the word. Men now see the hand-writing, and realize the certainty of judgments that are written against them, and they are "affrighted." For a little moment they cease from their blasphemies, "and give glory to the God of heaven" (v. 13). But it is not for long. It is the same mental and spiritual condition that is described at the close of the sixth seal and the sixth trumpet.* The time is the same. The powers of heaven are shaken. "Men's hearts are failing them for for fear, and for looking after (expectation of R. V.) those things which are coming on the earth."† They are affrighted, and for a moment seemingly religious, but continue utterly and hopelessly Godless.

---

*6:12, &c. and 9:20, 21-   †Lu. 21:26.

V. 14.   *"The second woe is past."*   It synchronizes with the close of the first act * and also with that of the second.† It brings the Apostate Church and the rebellious world to the hour of judgment. They are aware of it, and intense alarm prevails.‡

We are thus brought to the beginning of the last half of Daniel's Seventieth Week. But three and a half years of the appointed time remains. The mystery of God is almost finished.

The 7th trumpet is now to be sounded, and "the third woe cometh quickly."

REVELATION 11:15, &C.

ACT IV. 11:15, &C.   12: TO 20:1-4.

Scene 1st.—Chp. 11:15, &c.

Location.—In heaven.

Dramatis Personæ.—The Seventh Trumpet Angel. The four and twenty Elders. The Living Creatures.

Time.—The beginning of the 2d half of Daniel's last week.

We are now at the beginning of the end. When the " 7th angel sounded, there were great voices in heaven"—a mighty out-burst of rejoicings. It is the same grand choir that

---

*3:14 &c.   †6: 12 &c, and 9:16 &c   ‡Lu. 21:26.

we read of in chapter 4: The number of
the elect is now completed. The Church of
the Redeemed is safe with its Lord. The
mystery of sin is almost finished, and therefore the multitudes of the heavenly hosts rejoice and are glad.

V. 15. The first cause assigned for their
rejoicing is, that "the kingdom of this world
is become the Kingdom of our Lord, and of
his Christ, and that he shall reign forever
and ever." (R. V.).

The earth heretofore, though divided up
among many nationalities, was virtually but
one kingdom. "The whole world lieth in
the evil one" (R. V.).* He is its God,† and
is in possession. He is its one head, and
gives his authority to whomsoever he wills.‡
And thus will it be after this. No matter
what the future subdivisions, it continues to
be one kingdom, but under Christ.||

V. 17. "*Thou hast taken to thee thy great
power,*" &c. This is another cause for
thanksgiving. When the Lord came to
earth he emptied himself of majesty and
power.§ He was then, and, for the purposes of his salvation, he has been ever
since, seeming weakness. The very abjects
have scoffed at him and he has remained

---

*1 John, 5:19. †2 Cor. 4:4. ‡Rev. 13:2. ||Dan. 7:14,
Lu. 1:32, &c. §Phil. 2:6, etc.

silent. They have spit upon him, and he
has answered to never a word.   But all this
is now of the past.   His purposes of grace
have been accomplished, and he is about re-
suming his "great power," and "he shall
reign forever and ever".

V. 18. "*The nations,*" &c., i. e. apostate Christian peoples, those leagued with
the Anti-christ.*   Their anger is in contrast
with the "wrath" of the Lord God Almighty.

"*The time of the dead,*" clearly those who
sleep in Jesus.   The first resurrection is for
them only.†   The time for their judgment
(in the sense of reward) has come.‡

"*The prophets,*" &c.   The Old Testament
church is included.   "Them that fear thy
name," is the one feature that distinguishes
them all.

"*Small and great.*"   The distinguished
and the inconspicuous.   There is a similar
antithesis in chapters 13:16, and 19:18.

This ends the doxology.   It is anticipative of the end which they ABOUT THE
THRONE know to be near at hand.

V. 19.   The opening of the temple of
God in heaven follows.   Perhaps the doxology and the opening may have been simul-

*Ps. 2:   †Rev. 20:5.   ‡Rev. 7:9, 20:4, &c.

taneous.   Opening is disclosing, making
known.   The Divine purposes are now revealed to principalities and powers in the
heavenlies.   Hence their doxology.   The
mystery of God is finished.   The putting
forth of his power, and the manifestations
of his glorious purposes, as declared to his
servants, the prophets,* will from henceforth
rejoice the hearts of his loyal subjects.   Even
Satan, who seems to be present,† sees the
end.   He knows that he is to be cast out,
that his time is short.

"*There were lightnings,*" &c.   These as
yet are limited to the heavenly scene.   They
are symbolic of the wrath (v. 18) that will
soon be poured out on Satan and his kingdom.

REVELATION, 12:

ACT IV. 11:15 &c., 12:to 20:1-4.
Scene 2d.—Chap. 12:
Location.—Partly in the heavenlies, and
partly on the earth.   The Seer continues to
occupy a position where he can command all
that passes in both locations.
Dramatis Personæ.—The woman clothed
with the sun.   The Man-Child.   The Dra-

---

*Rev. 10:7.   †Rev. 12:9, 12, 13.

gon. Michael and his angels. The remnant of the woman's seed.

Time.—The beginning of the last half of Daniel's 70th week.

Chp. 12: We here open on a new scene, the second in this IV. Act. The first closed with the representations of the temple of God opened in heaven, with its accompaniments of lightnings &c. (11:19). All that follows from the beginning of this twelfth chapter to verse five of fifteenth, we regard as in a measure parenthetic. The 7th trumpet sounds, but the vial angels do not at once come upon the scene. When the 7th seal is broken, we read that "there was silence in heaven about the space of half an hour."* It was suggested that this was a silence of preparation; so to speak, the shifting and re-adjusting of scenery, that the Seer might be the better prepared for the new series of events to be brought to his notice. So here. We are entering upon a new series of events. The previous histories will be continued. They will be resumed at their points of discontinuance. There will be the same characters, but they will appear in new forms, and under different circumstances. The Seer needs therefore much explanation that he may

---

*8:1.

recognize these old characters, and that he
may become thoroughly master of details.
For this purpose, there is just here a momen-
tary suspension of the onward movement of
the prophetic history.   The time for the
judgment has come, and the world is ripe for
it, and expects it.   The mission of the 7th
trumpet is to set in motion the vial-angels,
that the execution of this judgment may begin.   But the Seer must first be made to understand clearly the position of things, and
their relations to each other and to coming
events.   The Church, and the world powers,
and the unseen forces of darkness, will still
be the historic subjects to be unfolded to him.
But he must comprehend the exact position of
the Church at this time in its two-fold relation of visible and invisible.   He must also
take in the position of the world-power in
its assumptions, exaltations, and blasphemies.
The onward movement of the history is therefore suspended for this purpose.   The Temple being opened, the next event in order
would be the summons to the seven vial-
angels; but we must wait until we reach the
15th chp. before this summons is issued.
All between, from chp. 12: to 15:6, is therefore parenthetic, and for the most part explanatory and preparatory for the judgment
scene.   These chapters contain a succession

of symbols, pictures and explanations, that
are to the Seer, what the scenery, the costumes, and the varied artistic combinations
of our modern stage, are to us—helps to
the better understanding of what is said and
done by the actors.

V. I. There appears to the Seer "a
great wonder in heaven." The R. V. sub-
stitutes "sign" for wonder. It is the same
Greek (σημειον) that throughout the N. T. is
translated "miracle," and sometimes "sign"
in the sense of miracle. We prefer the
rendering of our old version — "wonder."
What the Seer beheld was no more a miracle
than the horses and horsemen of the other
visions. It was a symbolic representation.
The sight caused the Seer wonderment—as-
tonishment.

"*A Woman.*" A woman is the symbol of
the Church in its totality. It is also made
adaptive to the Church in whatever relation
we find it. As an Apostate Church, she is
a harlot,* as the faithful Church, she is the
the bride.†

The symbol now given us is a conception
surpassingly beautiful. It repays prolonged
study. "A woman clothed with the sun,
and the moon under her feet, and upon her

---

*Rev. 17:1, &c.   †Rev. 19:7.

head a crown of twelve stars." This is the
very impersonation of majesty and purity.
It is not of the earth. It far transcends any-
thing earthly. The imagination must feast
upon it, and the mind grow to it, and enlarge
itself, before it can realize its heavenliness.
The greatest of artists has made this his subject, and has given to the world a master-
piece. It is a beautiful painting; but beside the word-picture it is feeble. Who can
paint the Bride of Christ, but Christ himself, and this is His representation of her.

There can be no question that the true
Church, the sealed ones of all ages, is here
symbolized. Sun, moon, and stars are the
scources of light for our material world. By
Divine ordering, for its spiritual needs, this
true Church, is ordained the "light of the
world."* To represent this Church therefore as clothed and adorned with the sources
of physical light is appropriate and beautiful.

That this woman represents the true
Church, the sealed ones of Chp. 7:, and the
witnesses of Chp. 11:, is made apparent by
V. 17. Here we are told that "her seed ...
keep the commandments of God, and have
the testimony of Jesus." None but the true

---

*Matt 5:14.

Church can produce such children. We note also that on her head there is a crown of twelve stars, the symbolic number of the Church.* In striking contrast with the light adorned woman, are the gaudy earth-wrought trappings of the harlot sitting on the scarlet-colored beast,† and equally in contrast are the judgments that are awarded them.‡

V. 2. We interpret this symbol as representing the whole body of the sealed ones. As such this sun-clothed woman has ever been the guardian and witness of the truth, and the keeper and nourisher of God's children. At the time of the vision (the middle of Daniel's last week), and in the condition in which she is represented, she is in pain to deliver up all the children that she is at this time carrying. In the ages past her children have been removed one by one, and she has seen them thus pass on "to the general assembly and Church of the first-born, which are written in heaven."§ But now at one birth all her children are to be translated from earth to heaven. She is in expectancy of the event, and is awaiting it. She is feeling the pressure of the times. The powers of heaven are being shaken, and she realizes from passing events that the hour of "re-

---

*See p. 95. †17:4. ‡14:1, &c., & 17:16. §Heb. 12:23.

demption draweth nigh.''*   She cries therefore, and her cry is—''Come Lord Jesus,
come quickly.''

V. 3.   The seer's attention is diverted for
a moment from this sun-clothed woman by
another vision.   It is a source of equal wonderment to him.—''A great red Dragon.''
Verse nine designates him more fully, and
identifies him with ''the prince of the power
of the air ''—''the God of this world.''   He
is represented with the symbols that belong
to Daniel's last Beast,† and to the Beast of
chp. 13:1 &c.,—''having seven heads and
ten horns, and seven crowns upon his head.''
These symbols are regarded as indicating
complete world power, a power that belongs
to Satan. ''The kingdom of this world '' is as
yet his.‡   The Beast|| is but his representa-
tive.   When Pharaoh placed Joseph over the
land of Egypt, he put his ring on his finger,
and arrayed him in other insignia of his
royalty.§   So when King Ahasuerus would
honor Mordecai, he ordered him to be clothed
in royal apparel.¶   The seven crowned
heads, and the ten horns belong to Satan.
They are the insignia of his kingship over
this earth.   For his own purposes he transfers them to the Beast.   He makes him his

*Lu. 21:28.   †7:7, 8.   ‡Matt. 4:8, &c., 1 John 5:19.
||Rev. 13:1, &c.   §Gen. 41:41, &c.   ¶Esth 6:7.

Joseph over the land of Egypt. All the governments of this earth have ever been controlled by him, and have been given to whomsoever he will, and have been administered for the promotion of his interests. But to this last representative of this Beast-power, there will be transferred in a remarkable degree " his power, and his seat, and great authority."*

' *V. 4.* " *Stars*," as already stated, represent prominent persons. Here the stars are from heaven. They therefore represent prominent dignitaries of the visible Church. They are cast down to earth. The picture is wonderfully graphic. There are but three strokes of the brush—the Dragon, the sweep of his tail among the stars of heaven, and one-third of them cast to the earth. It points to an apostasy in the visible Church, brought about through the agency of Satan. At this moment in the prophetic history this apostasy comes to the full. We identify it with the apostasy under the 6th trumpet,† and which at this time takes shape under the earth-Beast.‡ The number cast down is the same as that destroyed under the 6th trumpet.‖ It is with his tail that the Dragon draws these stars of heaven

*13:2. †9:14, &c. ‡13:11, &c. ‖9:18.

from their high places and drags them down
to the earth.   With his tail, *i. c.* with his
"cunning craftiness",* and his "wiles",†
and his "lying wonders", and his "deceiva-
bleness of (concerning) unrighteousness".‡
These are the agencies by which he deceives
and draws down these stars to the earth—to
the substitution of philosophy, and science,
and culture, and such like worldly wisdom
(things of the earth), for the doctrine of God
in Christ.   And so, under the 6th trumpet,‖
we are told that the power of the apostasy
thus described, lies "in their mouth, and in
their tails".   These stars are first won from
their allegiance to the truth by the lies and
cunning craftiness (the tail) of the Dragon,
and then practice the same with success
upon others.

As children of light, can we not "discern
the signs of the times"?§   In "the higher
criticism" that undermines the authority of
God's word; in the cowardice that cringes
before an assumptive science; in the voices
heard in all our churches questioning, if not
openly denying, the doctrines of the Atone-
ment, of eternal punishment, and of a returning Lord; can we not by these, and
many similar indications, discern the sweep

---

*Eph. 4:14.   †Eph. 6:11.   ‡2 Thess. 2:10.   ‖9:19.
§Matt. 16:3.

of the Dragon's tail, that is beginning to bring to the earth the stars of heaven?

Successful in his wily schemes, and with his apostasy almost at its culmination, the Dragon turns his attention to those who have refused to be led captive by him at his will. He is now seen standing before the woman anticipating the coming birth, and determined to devour the man-child to be brought forth. It will be noticed that the symbols we are now studying take us back in a measure over some of the historic ground we have already traversed. Under the 6th trumpet* we have the apostasy here symbolized by the Dragon's tail drawing the stars from heaven, and casting them down to earth. In chp. 11: there are the sackcloth-witnesses corresponding to the sun-clothed woman crying for deliverance. And in the statement of v. 5—"And her child was caught up unto God, and to his throne," we recognize the call of chp. 11: v. 12, " Come up hither." The translation, as we think, is shadowed forth in both instances. This repetition seems to be required, not only for the unity of the pictures, but that the continuity of the historical events should be perfectly clear to the seer.

_____

*9:14, &c.

The woman—the true Church, is crying and waiting for deliverance, This moment of her anguish may correspond to the three and a half days of the "dead bodies" of the witnesses lying unburied in the streets of Jerusalem.* The Dragon is seen watching for the birth of the child, with the avowed purpose of devouring it. Up to this time he seems to have had access in-to the heavenlies.† He has not yet been expelled. But he knows that "the end" is near,‡ and that his time is short. His wrath therefore knows no bounds, and in the madness of despair he seems to enter-tain the hope that it may be in his power to frustrate this translation—the Church delivering up her Man-child. In the symbol of the 6th trumpet,‖ the number of the horsemen (the heresies) sent forth was immense. It must be by these that he hopes to devour the Man-child—to tear the Bride, or at least a portion of her, from the Bridegroom.§

V. 5. The woman brings "forth a Man-child, who was to rule all nations with a rod of iron."—"She was delivered of a Son, a Man-child, who is to rule," &c., (R. V.).

---

*Rev. 11:8, †12:9. ‡12:13. ⸰John, 10:28. etc., 6: 37-41. ‖9:16.

Who is this Man-child?   Expositors in general agree in making him Christ.   The fact that he was to rule all nations, &c., seems to point to Him, and to none other.   But there are serious objections to this view.   To make the Man-child Christ, is to make the Church His Mother.   This has no warrant in scripture.   The Lord-christ, as to his humanity, was born of a woman.*   This was after the flesh.   The Church as here symbolized, is a woman not after the flesh.   She is heavenly and spiritual.   The children she nourishes for eternal life have received a spiritual birth. In no sense can Christ be said to have received a spiritual birth, or any other kind of birth, from, or in, or through, the Church.   He was begotten of the Father before all worlds. He is the Maker and the Organizer of the Church.   The Church is ''his body,'' ''his Bride,'' but not his Mother.   To make her his Mother is to make the less contain the greater.   It was not until after his birth, and even until after his death, that the Church had its being.   It is more correct therefore to say that Christ gave the Church being, than that she gave Him birth.   We must not interpret a symbol in a way plainly repugnant to the letter

*Gal. 4:2.

of scripture.   We cannot therefore accept the generally received intepretation that the Man-child is Christ.   We take it to be—all on earth at this special time, who are in Christ and who are waiting for him.   That the singular number—"a Son, a Man-child," should be used when numbers are concerned is quite in accordance with scripture usage. The words, Church, bride, body, are singular, and yet they stand for the whole number of the redeemed.   In his message to Pharaoh, God says: "Israel is my son, my first-born."* And so of Ephraim, he asks: " Is Ephraim, my dear son? is he a pleasant child?"†   All true believers are in Christ, and are one with him.   What is said of him is true of them. They shall reign with him.   The Angel tells Daniel " that the kingdom and dominion, and the greatness of the kingdom under the whole heaven, shall be given to the people of the saints (the Man-child) of the Most High." ‡And observe that the child is no sooner born than it is "caught up unto God, and to his throne."

We take the interpretation to be this.   The true Church on earth at this particular time is represented as delivering up her child "the

---

*Ex. 4:22, 23.   †Jer. 31:20.   ‡Dan. 7:14, 27, Matt 19:28. Lu. 22:29, 30.   Rom. 8:17, &c. I Cor. 6:3.   Rev. 2:26, 27, 3:21.   20:4, 6.

seed . . . to whom the promise was made."*
It is done at once, "in a moment, in the twinkling of an eye." It is the mystery of the
translation which has been revealed to us in
1 Cor. 15:51, &c., and still more fully explained in 1 Thess. 4:17, &c. It is the parable of the ten virgins in symbol. It is the
object lesson given us in Rev. 11:11 &c.

V. 6. The sun-clothed woman—the invisible and true Church, does not give up all
her children. The Man-child being taken up,
i. e. all in Christ who at the moment of the 7th
trumpet's sounding, are found watching and
waiting for the Bridegroom,† being caught
up, the woman will still be on the earth.
"Their enemies beheld them" is the statement in Chp. 11:12. The removal of so
great a number must attract universal attention. It must be accounted for and there
is only one way. The despised Book that
has been branded by the wisdom of the
world as a myth and a fraud, will speak and
will not lie. The consternation for a short
while will be great. Many will give glory
to God, and there will be believers added to
the Church of such as are being saved.
All of the ten watchers are spoken of as
virgins (true believers), though five are fool-

---

*Gal. 3:19.   †Matt. 25:1 &c.

ish. They have not heeded their Lord's warning,* and are therefore excluded from the marriage feast. They return, however, with oil in their lamps. These are spoken of in V. 17 as "the remnant of her seed, which keep the commandments of God and have the testimony of Jesus Christ." The sun-clad woman will therefore still be on the earth. But she has to "fly into the wilderness, where she hath a place prepared of God; that they should feed her there a thousand two hundred and three score days"—3½ years. The Dragon having failed in his designs on the Man-child, will, in his desperation, wage a war of extermination upon the remnant of her seed (V. 17).

"*The Wilderness.*" Many understand by this some special hiding place. We would eliminate the idea of place, and regard it as such general protection as the Lord has vouch-safed to his Church during times of persecu-tion. There always has been suffering and martyrdom, but he has never allowed exter-mination. This remnant of the woman's seed that will now be left within the visible Church and in the world, will be like the seven thousand hidden ones in Elisha's day.†

There is here a note of time. It is the

----

*Lu. 21:36.   †I. Kgs. 19:18.

same as that assigned to the sackcloth witness.* This difference however must be
noted. With them it is the first half (1260
days) of Daniel's last week, and prior to the
translation. Here it is the last half of the
week, and after the translation (V. 5). All
after the 7th trumpet, and the translation,
belongs to the last half of Daniel's week.

Vs. 7-10. The war in heaven, the expulsion of Satan, and his flight to earth, are to
us realities. Believing in the personality of
Satan, and of all concerned in this conflict,
and knowing that earth is a place, and that
heaven must be also, we can find neither
figure nor symbol in this language. We take
it literally.

This is the beginning of Satan's progress
towards his final destination. He is first expelled from heaven (Vs. 8-9); then he is seized,
and bound, and locked up in the bottomless
pit (20:1, &c.); and last of all he is cast into
the lake of fire.† Was this struggle we are
now considering and its result present to the
Lord's mental vision when he said—"I
beheld Satan falling as lightning from
heaven?" R. V.‡

V. 10. There is here given the Seer another of those explanatory voices helpful to

---

*11.3. †20:10. ‡Lu. 10:18.

him in understanding what is taking place.
This loud voice is probably from one or perhaps more, of the redeemed, for it speaks of
"our brethren."

V. 11.   "*They overcame Him because of*"
(R.V.).   Through ($\delta\iota\alpha$), by virtue, on account
of, "*the blood*" &c.   They were not
ashamed of the cross of Christ.   They accepted the doctrine of the efficacy of the
blood, and bore their testimony to it.   Without its shedding the accusations of the ad-
versary could not have been answered.

V. 12.   "*Woe to the inhabiters of the
earth and the Sea!*" &c.   This is the third
and last woe.* It is the "great tribulation."†
It will be upon Israel,‡ and upon the remnant of the woman's seed,§ and upon all na-
tions.|| It is to be on "the inhabiters of the
earth and the sea"—the dominion of the sea-
Beast, and   the followers   of the   earth-
Beast.

V. 13.   What follows to the end of the
chapter is both an amplification and an explanation of the statements of Verse 6th.
The events are, however, presented from different standpoints.   The first is the heavenly
aspect of the woman's flight.   The other**

---

*8:13.   9:12.   11:14.   †Matt. 24:15 23.   Dan. 12:1.
‡Jer. 30:7.   §V. 17. ||Lu. 21:25.   **Vs. 13 17.

gives the same facts with the fuller details, and is an earth-picture. We now learn why the woman had to fly into the wilderness—the Dragon has been cast out of heaven and is persecuting her.

V. 14. "*To this woman were given two wings.*" The upbearing, overshadowing, over-ruling, providence of God, that causes "all things to work together for good to them that love God, to them who are called according to his purpose."*

"*She is nourished.*" The same Greek that in V. 6th is translated "feed." The oil will be supplied that these lamps may continue burning† through all these 1260 days, so that when Christ comes there will be a true Church (the remnant of her seed) upon the earth.

Vs. 15, 16. These symbols are very difficult of explanation. "The serpent casts out of his mouth as a flood" &c. We are disposed to link this with 16:13, 14; and 9:16 &c. With "damnable heresies"‡—the immense army of horsemen of Chp. 9:16, he will endeavor to sweep away the remnant of the seed as with a flood. The earth-Beast, who will be at the head of these horsemen seems to

---

*Rom. 8:28.   Ex. 9:4.   Deut. 32:11 &c.   Ps. 63:7.
†11:3 &c.   ‡, 2 Pet. 2:1.

symbolize the same fact that is here announced.

V. 16. We have not seen, nor can offer a satisfactory explanation of this symbol. As the time for its fulfillment approaches, there will be more light.

V. 17. This verse is explanatory of verse 13. It tells why the Dragon persecuted the woman.

This closes our second scene. In it, the translation, which had previously been brought to the Seer's notice by other symbols, is reaffirmed. The defeat and expulsion of Satan from heaven to earth is pictured to him. The fact is also revealed that after the translation there will still continue to be a true Church upon earth. And he is made to understand the condition of the untranslated Church—the remnant of the woman's seed, down to the end of the 1260 days.

Act, IV. 11:15, &c., 12:to 20:1-4.

Scene, 3d. Chp. 13:

Location. The earth.

Dramatis Personæ. The Dragon. The sea-Beast. The earth-Beast. The inhabiters of the earth.

Time. The last half of Daniel's last week.

This scene opens with a vision very different from the previous one. That was a woman clothed in light, this is a Beast "scarlet-colored,"* fierce, cruel and impious. That was a heavenly picture pure and beautiful; this is of the earth earthy. We at once identify him with Daniel's last "dreadful and terrible" Beast.† He comes on the stage of action fully equipped for an awful work. Satan is now upon earth. Keeping himself out of sight for the better success of his lying doctrines, he will transfer to this Beast his "power, and his seat, and great authority," and he shall make war with the saints and overcome them. Contemporary with him is another Beast that comes up out of the earth. He is lamb-like, but speaks great swelling words. He exercises spiritual power over the nations, and is confederate with the

---

*17:3: †7:7.

sea-Beast.   By them the earth is subdued, and brought into a state of open and reckless rebellion against the Most High.

V. I.   The R. V. translates—"*and he (the Dragon) stood upon the sand of the sea. And I saw a Beast*" *&c.*   With the rising of this Beast, the Dragon ceases to occupy the conspicuous position that he did in the last scene.   He hides himself in this Beast, as he did in the serpent in Eden.   He gives him "his power, and seat, and great authority." This Beast comes up out of the sea—out of the disturbed civil and social relations of the peoples.*   It is out of the same sea that Daniel saw his Beasts arise.†   The Greek is θηφεον, a wild beast; very different from ἔωα, the living ones, of Chp. 4:6.

V. 2.   This Beast is nondescript.   He is a combination of those of Daniel, and thus shows his unity in spirit and purpose with those who have preceded him.   He symbolizes the aggregate of the empires of this world as opposed to Christ.

This Beast has "seven heads, and ten horns, and upon his horns ten crowns, and upon his heads the name of blasphemy (V. I.).   There is a still further descriptive allusion to him in Chp. 17:8 to 13.   We will bring together

---

*Rev. 17:15.   †7:2.

these statements, and give what seems to us a
possible explanation.

The seven heads in Chp. 17:9, are said
to be "seven mountains," and in the next
verse, these mountains are said to be "seven
Kings R. V.). The seven heads, and seven
mountains, and seven kings, are one. They
are intended to represent ruling powers. The
seven mountains may perhaps represent the
the different forms of government peculiar to
these heads, or Kings. Because the City of
Rome is built on seven hills, most expositors have inferred that the reference is to that
City, and to the Church of Rome—"the seven
heads are seven mountains, on which the
woman sitteth."* But this sitting of the
woman upon these seven heads, which are
seven mountains, does not imply possession,
and control, and sovereignty. Just the contrary. The reference is to the tableau of V.
3,—a woman sitting upon a scarlet-colored
beast (Chp. 7:). The Beast referred to is *carrying* the woman (V. 7.). Her sitting on him denotes a condition of dependence. He is be-
friending her—sustaining her in her position,
whatever that may be, and as these seven
heads, which are mountains, represent the
same Beast,† the relations of the woman to

*17:9. †13:1, &c.

them must be the same,—one of dependence.

The interpretation given the mountains, as
standing for forms of governments, finds ample authority in scripture. (Dan. 2:35. Heb.
12:22, and Rev. 14:1. Is. 2:1 &c. 41:15.
Ps. 68:15-16. Ezek. 35:1, &c.)

This Beast has also ten horns.* The horn
is the symbol of power, and ten is considered
the number of the complete course of the
world—the completed development of world-
power.† These horns wear crowns, the symbol of imperial power. This number ten is
linked with all the symbols of this world-
power. You find it in the ten toes of the
great image, and in the ten horns of Daniel's
last terrible Beast.‡ The Roman Empire
continued an unit throughout the first four
centuries. It was then divided into the East-
ern and Western Empires, the two legs of
Nebuchadnezzar's image. Since then, the ter-
ritories and nationalities it dominated, have
been broken up and subdivided again and
again. But there has always been more or
less adhesion and sympathy under a common
system of government—imperialism. The
idea of unification has never been lost sight
of. Its realization has been the ambition of

---

*13:1, &c., and 17:7, 12. †Lange on Rev. p. 316. ‡7:7

many who from time to time have deluged
Europe with blood.   These ten imperial
horns are yet future.   In 17:12, they are
said to be "ten Kings, which have received
no Kingdom as yet, but, they receive authority as Kings, with the Beast for one hour."
(R. V.) They correspond to the ten toes of
the image; and in Daniel's vision of the
Beasts, they are assigned to the fourth Kingdom, and to its last end, and as the Beast
(little horn) is to come up among these horns,*
we know that he belongs to the last Kingdom, and to the last end of that Kingdom.

In explaining "the mystery"† of this Beast,
the Seer tells us (13:3): "and I saw one of
his heads as it were wounded to death; and
his deadly wound was healed." And in 17:8,
he is spoken of as "the Beast that was,
and is not, and yet is," or, as the R. V.
translates, "he was, and is not, and shall
come."   This is still further explained in Vs.
10 and 11. "There are seven Kings (govermen-
tal forms); five are fallen, and one is, and the
other is yet to come . . . . and the Beast that
was, and is not, even he is the eighth, and
is of the seventh."

"*There are seven Kings, five are fallen.*"
We have interpreted these Kingships to be

*Dan. 7:8.   †17:7.

different forms of government through which this Beast-power passes. Following this line of interpretation we know from history that the Roman power up to Apocalyptic times had numbered six different forms of government—(1), Kings; (2), Consuls; (3), Dictators; (4), Decemvirs; (5), Military Tribunes. These at the time of the Seer had passed away,—" *five are fallen.*" (6) Emperors.* This was the form of government existing at the time the revelation was given,—"*One is.*" "*The other (the Seventh,) is not yet come.*" It was future in John's day. We regard it as still future. Although the Roman Beast-power in its imperial form no longer exists as an unit, yet in its fragmentary portions the monarchical form has almost universally prevailed. We may regard therefore the imperial (the 6th) form of the Beast power as still existing.

What then is this seventh and still future form? Let us note some of its features. (1)It was at the time of the Seer's writing still future.* When it comes, the Beast that was (before it), i. e, the imperial form of government, will receive a wound unto death,† Mrg. "was slain." (3) On its coming, it is to "continue a short space."‡

We are disposed to think that there is
coming an era of lawlessness that will sweep
the Roman world, and that will upturn its
thrones.　And it is well for those who rest on
the most sure word of prophecy to observe
"the signs of the times."　Clouds are thick
and threatening on the horizon, and it will
be our fault if the storm bursts upon us un-
awares.　The wonderful progress of science,
the rapid increase of knowledge, the cheer-
ing successes of missions, the growing influence of Peace Congresses—this promising
outlook makes optimists of us all.　But we
are assured that "when they shall say peace
and safety, then sudden destruction cometh,
.　.　.　and they shall not escape."* A spirit
of unrest and dissatisfaction is brooding over
the civilized world.　It is attracting the attention of all thinkers.　You read of it in
the columns of the newspapers, and the page
of the magazine, the quarterly, and the
novel.　Everywhere the question is asked—
how can we allay this threatening spirit?　It
is organizing and combining under manifold
names.　They are all more or less the outgrowth of atheism, and lead to lawlessness.
When men discard the fear of God, and the
expectation of an after life, and a righteous

---

*1 Thess. 5:3.

judgment, they also break the bond of human brotherhood, and discard all the elements that combine to form a perfect civilization. Self becomes the center of all action. And it is this fashion of atheism that is now taking possession of men's minds, and that needs only time to bring about the awful catastrophy, out of which the Anti-christ will be developed. The resisting influences of religion are being rapidly taken out of the way.* It was so in France in 1790. There was first a widespread infidelity nursed by men of letters. Society was corrupted, confidence and truth fled. Licentiousness was given free rein. Wealth and power combined to extort and oppress, and poverty and ignorance roused itself for resistance. Then came the upheaval; and the monarchy, and all that was law abiding, vanished. The same results must follow like conditions. Now, however, on a more extended scale. The whole world is one. Revolutions can no more be confined to nationalities. The great questions of the day are agitating the minds of men throughout the civilized world. When they come to be settled, there will be no German, no Frenchmen, no Englishmen, &c. The oppressor and the oppressed will

---

*2 Thess. 2:7.

stand face to face. And then will be the days when "there shall be signs in the sun, and in the moon, and in the stars; and upon the earth distress of nations, with perplexity; the sea and the waves (the uprising masses) roaring; men's hearts failing them for fear, and for expectation of those things which are coming on the earth for the powers of heaven shall be shaken."*

This era of lawlessness and bloodshed is that of the seventh head—the seventh form of government. It is mob sovereignty,— democracy run mad. In its wild frenzy all thrones will be overturned, all established principles of civil law abrogated, all recognition of religion prohibited, all safeguards to person and property broken down, and anarchy and terrorism will reign supreme. Thus a deadly wound will be inflicted on one of the heads of the Beast. The long estab lished monarchical form of government that has always characterized it, will be slain, and to all appearance—forever.

But this wild out-burst of passion will soon subside. The fury of so fierce a storm must spend itself quickly. It was so during the French revolution. Its "reign of terror" ran its course in 426 days. The people were

---

*Luke 21:25, 26.

satiated with blood, and there came a re-
action.   The first one strong enough to grasp
the reins and restore social order and personal
security, was hailed as a savior, and so will it
be here.   We are told—"*He*," this seventh
head, "*must continue a short space*" V. 10.
The strain will be too great for long continuance, "And except those days should be
shortened, there should no flesh be saved;
but for the elect's sake those days shall be
shortened."*   Humanity will long for deliverance, and will be ready to welcome any
one who will come in the name of law and
order, and so the next head (the eighth)
"*is of the seventh*," (V. 11.)   "The four
winds of the heaven"† have been striving on
the great sea, and from the midst of its roaring tossing waves‡—the madness of the peoples, this 8th head appears.   He will restore
the ancient regime.   The monarchial principle will once more appear, and thus "this
deadly wound is healed; and all the world
wondered after the beast.§   It will recognize
him as its deliverer, and will readily yield to
him all the power and honor he claims, even
to worship; and this beast that was, and is
not, and that is to come, is the eighth head.∥
and this is the Anti-christ.

*Matt. 24:22.   †Dan. 7:2.   ‡Lu. 21:25.   Rev. 13:1
§13:3.   ∥17:8, 11.

John tells us that there were even in his day,
many Anti-christs.*   A person, or organization, that in any way detracts from the authority and glory of Christ, manifests the
spirit of Anti-christ, and there are many such
in the world.   In this sense we may regard
the Church of Rome as Anti-christian; but
she is not *the* Anti-christ.   There is but one
such.   John thus describes him in one of his
epistles.   "Who is the liar, but he that
denieth that Jesus is the Christ?   This is the
Anti-christ, even   he   that   denieth   the
Father and the Son (R. V.)†   Rome has
never   denied the   divinity of   the Lord,
nor   his   mission.   She   is   not   therefore
the Anti-christ.   We must look elsewhere for
him, and it is in this 8th head—this last
development of Gentile Dominion that we find
him.   "He goeth into perdition."‡   "Whom
the Lord shall consume with the spirit of his
mouth, and shall destroy with the brightness
of his coming.|| He has   no successor.   He
is taken, and is "cast alive into the lake of
fire that burneth with brimstone (R. V.)§
With him the image is broken to pieces, and
becomes like the chaff of the summer thresh-
ing-floors, that the wind carries away.¶   The
mighty power which Satan energized, and by

*I John, 2:18. †I. John, 2:22. ‡17:8 and 11, ||2 Thess.
2:8. §9 Rev., 20. ¶Dan. 2:35.

which he dominated over the earth since the days when Nebuchadnezzar dreamed his dreams, and which has at last culminated in the "little horn," will now be taken away. "The judgment shall sit, and they shall take away his dominion, to consume and to destroy unto the end."* He is the desolator, and on him will be poured the determined consumation.†

We now confine ourselves to chapter thirteen.

V. 5. In this verse there is a note of time. The power of this Beast, as now represented by its 8th head, is to continue forty and two months—3½ years. It is the same period as Daniel assigns to his "little horn," and to his "Prince."‡ It is also the time allotted for the treading down of "the Holy City," and named for the sackcloth witnesses, and the woman's wilderness life.§

V. 7. *"Power was given him"* &c. This is by the Dragon.‖ It must be remembered that this power is permissive. God is over all. He controls in the armies of heaven and upon earth, according to the good pleasure of his will. What ever Satan may accomplish is by his permission. If he makes war with the saints, and overcomes

---

*Dan. 7:8-26. †Dan. 9:27. ‡7:25, 9:27. §Rev. 11:2, 3. 12:6, 14. ‖13:2.

them, divine purposes are being accomplished, and all things are working together for the good of them who love God. We need not fear the powers of evil. Their destructiveness is under control. Johovah God says to their assumptions and their madness—" Hitherto shalt thou come, but no further ; and here shall thy proud waves be stayed."*

This bestowment of power will explain why the Beast will be able to gather so vast an army for the last struggle.†

V. 9. This is a summons to give attention. It takes us back to 2:7, and 3:6, 13, 22. The call in these chapters is addressed to the Churches. The inference is therefore that the same parties are here intended.

V. 10. These will be times of persecution, and the temptation to the Church—the remnant of the woman's seed, will be to meet violence with violence—to resist with carnal weapons. The warning given them, is that in this Satanic war, they are not to take the sword in self defense. This is not the way God wants his people to resist the devil.‡ That the Beast overcomes them is by permission.§ And it is by the spirit of passive suffering for Christ, that the patience and faith

*Job. 38:11.   †Rev. 16:14. 17:12, etc. 19:19.   ‡Matt. 26:52, 53. 10:23.   John, 18:11.   Rom. 12:19.   § John, 19:11.

of the saints is manifested to the world. "In your patience possess ye your souls."*

V.11. "*Another Beast.*" This the earth-Beast. Verse one describes to us the coming up, and appearance and nature of the sea-Beast. He rises out of the political and social storms that agitate the people (the sea). He is the last head of the material World-forces, whose history has been given us under the seals. Now we have the earth-Beast—"He comes up out of the earth." This, we think, is "the wisdom of the world"—its culture, civilization, and humanitarianism. The Apostle James says of it—"it descendeth not from above, but is earthly, sensual (or natural), devilish."† It represents the spiritual World-forces. They were brought to our notice under the trumpets. The sixth trumpet shows them to us a great company of horsemen (heresies) spreading themselves over the earth and destroying.

Here we have these forces organized under a head, who is all-conspicuous. In the trumpet scene "the horsemen"‡ absorb all attention. In this symbol, their leader—the earth-Beast, is the one absorbing object of consideration. He is "the False Prophet of Chps. 16:13, and 19:20. His lamb-like ap-

---

*Lu. 21:19.   †3:15.   ‡9:16, etc.

pearance,—"he had two horns like a lamb"
(5:6), and indeed the whole character of his
career, has convinced all expositors that this
symbol represents a spiritual power.

"*He spake as a dragon.*" His lamb-like
appearance and dragon utterances bespeak
his true character—a false prophet, a lying
teacher, an emissary of the Dragon. This
corresponds with the Lord's description of
false prophets, which come to you in sheep's
clothing, but inwardly they are ravening
wolves.* He is innocence and benevolence
itself in his professions and apparent objects
—having the form of godliness; but there is
uncompromising enmity in his heart against
the Lord, and his annointed.†

Because of these prophetic characteristics
so conspicuous in this Beast, there is much
unanimity among the commentators in identifying him with the Papacy. But we see
more clearly in this symbol the impersonation
of the spiritual and intellectual forces of the
world. It is the product of Protestantism
rather than of Romanism. Romanism
cramps, binds, enslaves. Protestantism in-
culcates individual responsibility, and intellectual freedom; and so emancipates Rome's
captives. And it is this emancipated intellect

---

*Matt. 7:15. †2d Pet. 2:1, &c. 1. Tim. 4:1, &c. 2. Tim.
3:1, &c. 4:2, &c.

broken loose from "the wisdom that is from above" and captivated and enslaved by that which is "from beneath," that it seems to us to be here represented. We are disposed therefore to regard this Beast as entirely distinct from Rome. Rome finds its symbol in the Harlot-woman of Chp. 17: That it is not Rome is clear from the different relations they occupy to the sea-Beast, and also in the different destinies. Rome, the Harlot-woman, is to be carried—"upheld and sustained, by the sea Beast and his ten Kings, and at last is to be destroyed by them.* But this earth-Beast is to be confederated with the sea-Beast. He will be an efficient and indispensible helper, and they two shall meet the same judgment, and go into perdition together.†

We regard this symbol then, and also that under the 6th trumpet, as *apostate Protestantism*. It is not improbable that at this crisis, Protestantism will melt away. There is no adhesion about it. The intellectual freedom that is one of its underlying principles, is also one of its chiefest elements of disintegration. Rome will stand the shock, for a while at least. Its adhesive qualities are great. It is the most adaptive, and at

---

*17:3, 16.   †19:20.

the same time powerful, government the world has ever seen. It can fight fire with fire. But in this hour of evil's supremest triumph, our boasted Protestantism will probably vanish. Its best elements will hide themselves in the dens and caves of the earth—the remnant of the woman's seed will be in the wilderness; and the rest—the great mass of it, will be the multitude of armed horsemen (heresies), swelling the train of this earth-Beast—the False-Prophet.

This is no fancy sketch. It is a fact too plainly shadowed forth on the pages of history. Protestantism is even now riddled through and through with false doctrine. It is undermining its foundation with its own hands. This is not, therefore, an exaggerated statement--that Protestantism will melt away. It is a logical conclusion, a self-evident fact. If Chillingworth's position is sound—''the Bible, and the Bible only, is the religion of Protestants,'' and it never has been questioned, then Protestantism rests on the Scriptures as the Word of God. Aside from them it has no foundation. It has neither traditions nor councils to guide, nor Church authority to fall back upon. Take away then our Bible, and our Protestantism must go. And this is what German theology with its so-called ''higher criticism'' is doing. It

is undermining the authority of the Scriptures as the Word of God by endeavoring
to prove that from the beginning to end they
are a fraud. And Protestantism loves to have
it so. This show of wisdom takes wonderfully. To be a learned man and a great the-
ologian, is to be able to throw doubt on every
important statement of the Word, and whereunto must this tend but to the rankest infidelity, and to the utter extinction of Protestantism. And the progress toward it is not
slow.

You see it in its doctrines of the Divine
Paternity, of future probation, conditional
immortality, and human perfectability; in its
Sabbath desecration, in spiritualism, in the
assumptions of science falsely so-called, in
Positivism, and Agnosticism, in Humanitarianism, and Theosophism, and in the name of
culture, the modernizing and revival of
Mohamedanism and the Ancient religions of
the East. All this is the outgrowth of
Protestant freedom of thought, and all these
heresiarchs have a common bond of union—
rejection of the scriptures as a Divine
Authority, and denial of the Lord who
bought them.*

V. 12.   "*He exerciseth all the power of*

*2 Pet. 1: etc.

the first Beast (the Beast of the Sea) *before him*, (i. e. in his presence, R. V.), *and he causeth the earth and them which dwell therein to worship the first Beast, whose deadly wound was healed*"—the eighth head. There is here a confedracy, a union between the world's power and its culture to promote a common end. It results in "the deification of nature and humanity." The miraculous powers accredited to both these Beasts are real. The power that is now witheld, will then be given through the Dragon.* The God of heaven will seem at this terrible moment to have abdicated his throne, and to have deserted his world.

V. 14. He makes "*an image of the Beast,*" &c. This sea-Beast will be the incarnation of world-power. Its pre-eminently distinguishing characteristic will be the denial of God and his Christ.† As Christianity has its cross, and Mahometanism its crescent, so this sea-Beast will have his symbol. It is the earth-Beast, the world's wisdom, culture, and art, that will devise and produce it, and recommend its adoption. It is probably this symbol (image) that the anti-Christ will erect in the holy place—"the abomination" spoken of by Daniel and the Lord.‡ We

---

*Matt. 24:24. 2 Thess. 2:9. †1 John 2:22. ‡Dan. 9:27. Matt. 24:15.

are also reminded of the great metallic image.*

V. 15. "*And he had power to give life,*" *&c.* These events are yet future. There must therefore be much that we cannot as yet even spell out. We must wait, Spiritualizing the language, we may give it this interpretation.—Everyone will be compelled to wear (v. 16) one of these images as an evidence of his acceptance of the damnable heresy on pain of consequences (v. 17), and so, for every man the image will have a living and speaking power for life or death. "*Should be killed.*" Science and "advanced thought" has already begun its ostracism upon those who adhere to the old doctrines of the cross.

Vs. 16 and 17. Here again we must wait until the time comes before we can know what this "mark" is. It is in contrast to the sealing of chap. 7:.

V. 18. Numerous attempts have been made to solve this problem of the Beast's number. Here, too, we must wait. Doubtless to those who will be most concerned, there will be given "wisdom." They shall know.

This is a woeful picture of Apostasy here presented. Such a state of things seems impossible from our present standpoint of

---

*Dan. 2:31, etc.

Church aggressiveness, and mission effort, and successful work. And we look at the interpretation given these symbols, and ask in amazement,—can these things be? Is it possible that there could be such an outbreak of evil amid our Christianization and civilization? Humanly speaking, it seems impossible, and the belief of the great body of the Church is against it. But we turn from this view of the seeming probability of things— from this worldly outlook, to the teachings of the word of God; and here we find the "sure word of prophecy" announcing this apostasy, and the Lord and his apostles forewarning concerning it. The Lord's command to disciples is to teach his Gospel among all nations. Their attitude is to be that of witnesses.* And while the Gospel is to be preached in all the world, it is nowhere said that it will convert the world. On the contrary, the testimony everywhere in the Book is, that along with the witnessing, and resulting from it, there will be opposition, hatred, persecution, and apostasy.† The mission of the Gospel among the nations during this dispensation is witnessing, not converting. It is to take out from among the nations a people for his name.‡ Indi-

---

*Lu. 24:48. Acts 1:8. †Matt. 24:4-14. ‡Acts 15:14.

viduals will be converted, but not nations. It is important to note this, lest the ardent missionary spirit now pervading the Church be chilled by results.   The Gospel's grand mission now is witnessing.*   And when the story of the cross has been told to all nations, and God's elect ones have been sealed, what then?   Why, "the end"—the revealing of "the man of sin"—the Anti-christ, with his assumptions and blasphemies ; an Apostate Church and world running after him ; a translated Church ; and wrath poured out. The Lord Christ will not come until after these events.   So at least an inspired apostle tells us: "Let no man deceive you by any means, for that day (the day of the Lord's appearing) shall not come, except there come a falling away first, and that man of sin be revealed, the son of perdition."†

REVELATION, 14:

Act. IV.   11:15 &c.   12:to 20:1-4.
Scene, 4th. Chp. 14:
Location.   In the heavenlies.
Dramatis Personæ. The Lamb. The 144,-000.   The announcing and executing angels. The Son of Man.

---

*Matt. 24:14.   †2 Thess. 2:3.

Time. The beginning of the last half of Daniel's last week.

The fourth scene opens on Mount Sion. It is a picture of the Church triumphant. The number of "the elect" is now completed, and as a completed Church, the Lamb and his 144,000 meet together for the first time. No wonder that they are joyous and that they make the heavens ring with their "new song." There never was in all the past when that song could have been sung before; there never will be in all the coming cycles when this song will not be sung.

The previous scene was on the earth, and was terribly earthy. This is in the heavens, and is heavenly. The two are strongly in contrast. They represent events that are transpiring at the same moment in the different localities. At the beginning of Daniel's last week, three and a half years before "the end," the two Beasts are at the height of their career, deceiving, blaspheming, persecuting, destroying; and the remnant of the woman's seed is being driven by the Dragon into the wilderness. This is on the earth. At the same time the Man-Child has been caught up unto God, and his throne. In the heavenlies, the Lord and his elect are gathered in a joyous and everlasting union; and before *The Throne*, and in the presence of the Living Ones, and the Elders, with harp and voice, they sing their "new song, and the shout of their triumph is as the voice of many waters, and as the voice of a great thunder."

This scene does not represent progressive events, or if so, to a very limited extent. Everything as we have suggested, in chapters 12: 13: and 14:, excepting the first five verses of chapter twelve, has a common starting point—the sounding of the 7th trumpet. The exact status in the heavens and on the earth at this instant of time, is, as it were, photographed, that the Seer might behold and understand the situation, and might write it out for the study of the future Church. The events pictured in 12:1-6, the birth of the Man-Child, his danger from the Dragon, and his being caught up to God (the translation), transpire just before the sounding of the 7th trumpet, and are the same as those represented in chapter 11:1-15. They are the last acts under the 6th trumpet. The 7th follows immediately. The re-introduction here* of the same events is explanatory. It is also necessary to the unity and beauty of the most beautiful of pictures. The pictures that follow, and that photograph the exact

*12:1-6.

conditions in heaven and earth the moment
after the 7th trumpet has sounded, are (1),
the Dragon expelled from the heavenlies, and
coming down to earth in great wrath (12:7
&c); (2), the woman having delivered up her
Child (the translation), fleeing with the remnant of her seed into the wilderness from the
wrath of the Dragon (12:6, 14 &c); (3), the
Beast of the sea (13:1 &c) energized by the
Dragon, exalting himself and beginning his
blasphemous career; (4), the Beast of the
earth (13:11 &c) taking form and by means
of the power given unto him, identifying
himself with, and greatly sustaining the sea-
Beast: (5), the Lamb and his 144,000
gathered on the Mount Sion in the heavenlies (14:1&c.) Such is the position of things
in the heavenly places and on the earth; immediately after the 7th Angel sounds; and so
they continue, modified by the circumstances
incident to the out pouring of the vials, during the next 3½ years—to "the end" the
pouring out of the last vial.

V. 1. In chapter 11:12 and 12:5, there
has been given us as seen from the earth,
the last glimpse of the translated ones. "They
ascended up to heaven in a cloud; and their
enemies beheld them." They were caught
up to God and His throne. Here is the next
scene. This is what followed immediately

after they were "caught up unto God."   In Matt. 25:10 &c., we are shown the outside of the shut door, and what took place without. Here we are privileged to look within.   We now see the trysting place and the banqueting hall, and we can feast our eyes and ears on what is there taking place.   The Bride is with the Bridegroom.   The Church triumphant is with its exalted head.*

"*The Lamb*" (R. V.)   This is the same who " is in the midst of *The Throne*,"† and who tends his people with a shepherd's care,‡ And it is also the same Lamb whose wrath is so terrible to his enemies.§

"*Mount Sion.*"   Where is it?   It is the "holy dwelling place" of the Most High, even heaven.‖

"*An hundred forty and four thousand.*" They are the same as those of chapter 7:4, 9.   They are also the witnesses of 11:12, and the Man-Child of 12:5.   They are they who through all the ages have "come out of great tribulation, and have washed their robes, and made them white in the blood of the Lamb."¶ They are the gathering together of two classes of saints—those who are asleep and those who at this moment of time are alive and yet in the flesh, and who shall be

*I. Thess. 4:14.   †5:6.   ‡7:9, 17.   §6:16 &c.   ‖2 Chron. 30:27.   Heb. 12:22, 23,   ¶ See p: 94.   7:14.

changed in a moment in the twinkling of an eye.* In the scene of the transfiguration, we have these two classes represented in the persons of Moses and Elijah. Moses, who died and was buried on the Mount; and Elijah, who was translated in the chariot of fire.

"*Having his name, and the name of his Father, written on their foreheads*" (R. V.) This is in contrast with those who have the mark of the Beast in their hands, and on their foreheads.†

V. 3. "*And they sung as it were a new song.*" This is the first time the conditions are such as to call forth this song. It was never possible before. The number of "the elect" is now completed. Up to this time it had been an incomplete and a divided Church, a part struggling on earth, a part waiting in heaven.‡ But now it is a completed, and an united body, its song is therefore possible, and possible for the first time. Israel could not sing their song of triumph until all had passed safely through the sea and were on the other shore,§ and it was only those who had been "redeemed from the earth" who could sing this song. "It presupposes the entire depth and circuit of their experience, and the whole

---

* 1. Cor. 15:51 &c.　1. Thess. 4:13, &c.　†13:16.
‡Rev. 6:9 &c.　§Ex. 15:

state of their being brought from the earth."*

Neither the Living Ones. nor the Elders, take part in this song. It is sung "before" them, i. e. in their presence. They cannot join in it. This is conclusive evidence that they do not symbolize the Redeemed Church.†

V. 4. These redeemed ones are designated by six marks.

(a) "They are virgins." The Greek word is applicable to men as well as to women. It is clearly used here in a spiritual sense—they have kept themselves from idolatry. In Chp. 15:2, we have this same company described as those who "had gotten the victory over the Beast, and over his image, and over his mark," etc. Whoredom and adultery are figures of constant occurrence in scripture to denote spiritual unfaithfulness. They are frequently used in connection with Israel.‡ Such is the condition of the Church in Thyatira.§ Paul hopes to present the whole Corinthian Church to Christ as "a chaste virgin."‖ So in Matt. 25: the Church is represented under the figure of ten virgins. In Chp. 7: this same company (the 144,000)

----

* Lange, Rev., p. 278. †See p. 59, &c. ‡Num. 25:1-4: Jer. 2:3: Ezek. 6:23: Hos. 1:3: §Rev. 2:20 &c. ‖2, Cor. 11:2.

are called "Israel." As the name "Israel"
has been there taken in a figurative sense, so
must we here regard the term "virgins." It is
used as the anthithesis of "harlot" in Chp. 17:
We have no question as to the symbolic meaning of "harlot" in that chapter, we need
have none as to the import of "virgins" here.*

(b) "*They follow the Lamb whitherso-
ever he goeth.*" This was the command
laid upon them while in the world, and as
they did it faithfully amid self denials, re-
proaches, and great tribulations, so will they
continue this following, as "the ransomed of
the Lord . . . with songs, and everlasting joy
upon their heads."†

(c) "*They were redeemed*" (purchased)
(R. V.).‡ "*From among men*"—"God did
visit the Gentiles, to take out of them a
people for His name."(Acts, 15:14. Rev. 7:9.)

(d) "*They are first fruits unto God*" &c.
"Every man in his own order: Christ the
first fruits, afterward they that are Christ's
at his coming"§ It includes all the Redeemed of all dispensations up to the time of
this gathering on Mount Sion.

(e) "*In their mouth was found no guile.*"
They were true in their allegiance and their
service. "Faithful even unto death."

---

*Ezek. 6:99.   † Is. 35:10.   Rev. 7:14 &c.   ‡1 Peter.
1:18 &c.   §1 Cor. 15:20, 23.

(f) "*They are without fault.*"   Their
qualities are summed up in this one word—
faultless. The promise has been fulfilled.
They have not only been kept from falling, but
they have been "presented *faultless* before the
presence of his glory with exceeding joy.''*
This is the Church that Christ loved, and for
which He gave Himself, "that he might
scanctify and cleanse it, with the washing
of water by the word; that He might present
the Church to Himself, glorious, not having
spot, or wrinkle, or any such thing; but that
it should be holy and without blemish.''†

Vs. 6 and 7.   We enter now upon a new
series. of visions.   Let it be remembered that
all these scenes are prior to the judgments.
The vial-angels have not yet started on their
mission of wrath.‡ All that we are now
considering, and that we have considered, is
initiative.   It is preparing the Seer to understand the better, the onward movement of the
history, with its succession of judgments,
when it shall be resumed.   We are now seeing from the heavenly stand-point. We have
witnessed the gathering of the 144,000 on
Mount Sion, their meeting with the Lamb,
and we have also heard the voice of their ex-
ultation.   They still occupy this position,

---

*Jude, 24.   †Eph. 5:25-28.   ‡Chp. 16:

and will continue to do so, until the King rides forth with his armies, and begins His grand movement towards the earth. The first of these visions that follow relates to the coming judgments. It pictures to the Seer three Announcing Angels. The first is the Gospel-preaching angel. "When the fullness of the time was come" for the first advent, angels announced the birth of the Son of Man; and later on, his messenger went before his face to prepare his way before him, and to proclaim that the kingdom of heaven was at hand. So now at this his second advent there doubtless will be ample warning given the Church and the World that they may prepare for his coming. The angel is seen flying "in the midst of heaven having the everlasting Gospel to preach," &c. The ascension of the witnesses* produces great consternation. The five excluded virgins will now have oil in their lamps. The remnant of the Woman's seed will unhesitatingly testify in behalf of their coming Lord, and there will be thus a general proclamation of 2d advent doctrines to all them that dwell on the earth.

V. 8. This is the second Announcing Angel. The burden of his message is—

---

*11:12, 13,

"Babylon is fallen." It has been decreed, and therefore in God's sight it is accomplished. Bear in mind that these scenes are from the heavenly stand-point. May we venture the suggestion that they are not only to help the Seer to a better understanding of coming judgments, but also the newly glorified Church, and even the living creatures, and the Elders. Satan is no longer present, and the Divine purposes are now, therefore, being unfolded with unwonted clearness to the angels, who desire to look into these things.

"*Babylon.*" The manner in which this judgment was executed is given more fully in Chp. 18.

There is a very general agreement that Rome is here symbolized by Babylon. We prefer seeing in the symbol the God-defying world-power of Gentile dominion. Babylon was the beginning of this world-power. It was the mother city, and is used therefore appropriately to represent its entire social and commercial systems to the end. Thus we speak of Rome as the representative of the religious system that centers there. So we make London, Paris, or any of the great capitals, stand for their respective countries, when we would speak of their policy, their commercial standing, &c.   (See p. 211, &c., and 217, &c.)

Vs. 9-11.   The third Announcing Angel here delivers his message.   It is one of warning.   It may be that these angels (messengers) signify a revival of Gospel preaching by the remnant of the woman's seed, and that their utterances indicate the burden of the message that shall then be delivered.   And if so, we learn that in that day the Church will not shrink from preaching concerning a coming Christ, a judgment, and a hell.

The Dragon will have cause to be wroth with the woman, and the two Beasts will make war with the saints.   They, therefore, that keep the commandments of God, and the faith of Jesus, will have need of patience. (V. 12.)

V. 13: "*Blessed are the dead which die in the Lord from henceforth.*"   From this time on to "the end"—from the beginning of this last half of Daniel's last week.   According to our scheme of interpretation, this is the period of these prophecies (11:15, &c.   And 12: 13: and 14:) that we are now considering.   In prophetic time we are standing just 3½ years from the time of "the end."   The translation is an accomplished fact.   The "great tribulation" is about beginning.   The remnant of the woman's seed is still upon the earth. During the continuance of these 3½ years their condition will be truly pitiable. The Dragon in his wrath is making such war upon them as he has never done before. Blessed are they who by a natural death are called away, and are thus spared this prolonged suffering during these 1,260 days.

V. 14. We have had the three Announcing Angels. We now have the three Executing Angels. The Lord Christ is at the head of these as he was at the head of the others. As the head of the first trio, he appears as the Lamb surrounded by his triumphant Church, because these announcements (of a preached Gospel and of Babylon fallen, and of wrath on the Beast-worshipers) are for his Church. His Church on earth possibly is to be his agent (his angels) in keeping these facts before the world. But now he appears in the majesty of judgment, and he is the "Son of Man" (Matt. 24:30. 26:64. 2 Thess. 1:7, &c.) These angels at his commanding, come forth out of the temple to execute wrath upon a world that will not be warned. (Matt. 13:30. Lange, on Rev. in loco.)

The fulfillment of these prophetic pictures is yet future. Any attempt at explanation must be only conjectural—guessing. They are an announcement of what is to come. The fact of the fulfillment is recorded in 17:16, and 18: and 19: 19, &c.

REVELATION 15:16:

ACT IV.   11:15, &c., TO 20:1–4.

Scene 5th.—Chp. 15:16:

Location.—Partly in heaven, and partly on earth.

Dramatis Personæ.—The Seven Vial-Angels. "Them that had gotten the victory." The Living Ones. The Unclean Spirits.

Time.—The last three and a half years of Daniel's last week.

It is still a heavenly picture we are considering. The drama, however, begins now to move on. At first sight this chapter (15) with its song of triumph and its opened temple, seems a repetition of Chp. 11:15, etc. It is rather a going back to that scene than a repetition of it. In that scene the temple of God was opened. It was just at this point that the digression began, and it is to this point that the seer is again brought (V. 5) that he may, as it were, take a fresh start. There are some new features here, *e. g.* the "seven angels having the seven last plagues," and the song, which is unmistakably that of the translated. But these be-

long legitimately to that first scene, and possibly were represented; but their narration
has been delayed until the explanations to
be given would make them more intelligible.

It was suggested that the onward movement of the prophetic history was interrupted at the close of Chp. 11. Then the
Temple of God had just been opened in
heaven. The object of this interruption was,
as stated, to give the seer an intelligent outlook of the heavenly and the earthly situation at the opening of this last half of
Daniel's Seventieth Week. All between, from
Chap. 12: to 15:6, we regarded as explanatory,
and intended to prepare the Seer for the
better understanding of the coming judgment scenes. For our own assistance let
us again recall these scenes.

(*a*) The Church in pain (because of persecutions), and ready to be delivered of her
Man-child 12:1, 2.

(*b*) A great apostasy. Vs: 3, 4.

(*c*) The translation. V. 5. After this,
the translated Church becomes a feature in
the pictures. These three events are just
prior to the 7th trumpet, or the beginning of
the last half of Daniel's Week. What follows is immediately after the trumpet sounds.

(*d*) War in heaven, and Satan cast down
to the earth. Vs. 7-10.

(*c*) Joy in heaven over the event.   Vs.
10–13.

(*f*) The woman flying into the wilderness.
and protected.   Vs. 6, 14.

(*g*) The wrath of the Dragon, and his
war on the seed, which continues to the end.
Vs. 13, 17.

(*h*) The starting on their career of the sea
and the earth-Beast.   Chp. 13:

(*i*) The Lamb and his Church triumphant
on Mount Sion.   14:1–16.

(*j*) The three Announcing, and the three
Executing Angels.   14:6, &c.

These are pictures that reveal to the Seer
the status of all the parties, who will be in
one way and another concerned or involved
in the coming judgments.   The whole is
preparatory. It is a mapping out of positions,
and a description of the coming actors.   It
is information, essential to the leader on the
eve of great events or conflicts.   The com-
mander-in-chief from some eminence is surveying his proposed battle field.   His aides
are about him.   Yonder he has massed his
infantry.   His cavalry are hidden away in
the valley.   The artillery occupies the ele-
vations.   He takes in the whole situation.
All is now ready.   It waits but the appointed
hour, and the word of command.   So here,
after these pictures have been shown him,

the Seer is able to take in and understand
the positions and relations of all the parties
concerned in this approaching conflict between the powers of good and evil.

And thus taught and prepared, the Seer,
in Chp. 15, is carried back to the initial
scene of the 7th trumpet* —the triumphant
song, and the open temple. This time,
however, the prophetic history moves on to
its completion.

V. 1. Reference is not made again to the
7th angel-trumpeter. He had sounded † and
all that follows is consequent upon it. We
had already been told of this opening of the
temple. That, together with the anthem of
the Angelic Hierarchy, is the first event that
follows this sounding. ‡ The next is this
appearance of these seven angels, § having
the last seven plagues. They come from
the Open Temple (V. 6) of Chap. 11:19.
Their procession is not mentioned when
we are first told of the opening of this
Temple, because the narration there, as we
have suggested, was interrupted for a while.
But here it is resumed, and just when this
course of events was interrupted. Between
verses 1 and 5, on a smaller scale, we have
a repetition of this parenthetical structure.

---

*11:15, etc. †11:15. ‡11:19. §15:1.

Verse 1 pictures the procession of the seven angels with their plagues. Verses 2, 3, and 4, give us the song of those who had gotten the victory over the beast; and verse 5 takes us back again to the temple scene of V. 1, and to the out-going angels. And thus it is after this larger interruption—the Seer is taken back in V. 1 (Chp. 15), and again in V. 5, to the same opened temple, he had seen in Chp. 11:19. And now from amid its lightenings, and voices, and thunderings, he beholds these seven angels coming out. The progress of the prophetic history is thus resumed, and all in between these two points * must be regarded therefore as parenthetical.

V. 2. These are clearly the redeemed ones—the whole Church of Chp. 14: Their song is not to be associated with that of the Living Ones, and the Elders of 11:15, etc. It is entirely distinct. To have introduced it when that first song was sung, would have been utterly confusing to the Seer. He would have been bewildered as at the Elder's question in Chp. 7:13, etc. But now that he has been shown the Man-child caught up to God, and Mount Sion with the Lamb and his 144,000, he has no difficulty in deciding

---

11:19, & 15:6.

who they are that sing this song of Moses and the Lamb.

The order of events seems to run thus. The seventh Angel sounds.* At once, amid the anthems of angelic hosts, the temple opens,† and the seven Angels make their appearance.‡ Then the ransomed ones take up the strain, and sing their song of Moses and the Lamb. §

V. 3. Moses was the agent of a deliverance that called forth a song of triumph from God's people. ‖ That was a type and fore-casting of this deliverance of God's Church, of which Christ is the author and the perfecter.¶

Vs. 5, etc. The opened temple, the issuing Angels, the living ones presenting them with the seven vials full of the wrath of God, no man suffered to enter the temple until these plagues shall be poured out—these things have their significance, but the time for their unfolding is not yet.

CHAPTER 16.

And now the last awful scene of the drama begins. Let us, even at the risk of too much repetition, go back a little, and take in as fully as we can the order and meaning of the symbols as we have been interpreting them.

---

*11:15.   †1:16-19.   ‡15:1 & 6.   § 15:2-5.   ‖Ex. 15. "Heb. 3:1-7.

The 7th seal contained the seven trumpets,* and the 7th trumpet contains the vials.† In the visions connected with the seals, we recognized the history of Gentile dominion (" the times of the Gentiles "), together with that of the Church (visible and invisible) in its relation to this dominion. Then in the symbols of the trumpets, we have presented the spiritual and intellectual world forces, and again the history of the Church (visible and invisible) is given, as it stands related to these forces. These histories synchronize. They have a common starting point, the cutting off of Messiah the Prince; and a common terminus at or about the middle of Daniel's last week — "in the midst of the week."‡ At the sounding of the 7th trumpet, § these histories are taken up again from this common point to which they had all been brought (the middle of Daniel's week), and they are continued to "the end." This 7th trumpet therefore ushers in the events of the last 3½ years in their relation to Gentile dominion and the Church. It was down to this point that the 6th seal and the 6th trumpet had brought them. Under this 7th trumpet there is given first of all, a description of the

---

*8:1, 2. †11:15 & 15:1. ‡Dan. 9:27. §11:15.

various actors* that are to be interested in any way in the coming events, whether in heaven, or earth, or under the earth. And what an array of visible and invisible forces they are! Man is but a puppet to be moved at their pleasure, and to be crushed by their power. All these forces are marshaled before the Seer. He is placed in a position where he can at a glance command every movement; and when everything is so explained that he can take in intelligibly all that will transpire, then the great movement connected with this 7th trumpet begins. —The sealed ones are on Mount Sion; they are safe, having escaped those things that are coming on the earth: The Anti-christ has taken his Dragon-given seat, and has started on his career of conquest and of blasphemy, upheld by the earth-Beast, and the Harlot-woman: the earth is ripe for vengeance:† the messengers of wrath are commissioned, ‡ and the command given them § to go their ways: the Angels of Chp. 7:1, etc., are no longer restrained, and "the four winds" are loosed, and now rush on earth, and sea, and trees, an overwhelming storm. And this time it is not man's wrath; but "the wrath of the Lamb;

---

*11:15 &c. to 15:1-6. †14:15. ‡15:6. §16:1.

for the great day of his wrath is come; and who shall be able to stand?"*

V. 1. The third and last woe is come. † It is the Anti-christian night of the world. Its last hour, and its darkest, because it just preceeds the dawn—the Parousia.

If our theory of interpretation is correct, we. are dealing with last things, and consequently with things future. It is impossible therefore to conjecture the nature of these plagues.

In connection with the seven trumpets, and the seven vials under them, Bp. Elliott calls attention to the taking of Jericho, the fall of the first city that obstructed Israel's entrance into Canaan. The Israelites marched around the city once for six successive days, blowing their trumpets; on the seventh day they compassed it seven times. "It almost seems," says Elliott, "as if some power were marked out hereby as the N. T. Jericho, whose domination opposed and whose overthrow would introduce the Saints' enjoyment of the heavenly Canaan."‡

V. 2, &c. The vials are poured out upon the earth, sea, rivers, fountains, air. All nature becomes disjointed. What was the life and happiness of man now turns against

*6:16,17. †11:14. ‡Lange, on Rev., p. 213.

him. Note the rapidity with which the vials follow each other. The Lord is making quick work of it. He will execute his judgments speedily.

V. 6. *"For they have shed (poured out R. V.) the blood of saints" &c.** "Blood to drink." They shall be satiated with slaughter, *e. g.*, as during the French revolution.

V. 7. *"And I heard the Altar, saying"*, &c. R. V. Perhaps those who cry in Chp. 6:9, &c.

Vs. 10-11. Cf. 9:20, 21. The source of this delusion that could thus harden their hearts and drive them to defiance against the power that was crushing them, is to be found in verse 14. See also 17:12–15, and 19: 19.

V. 13. *"Three unclean spirits,"*—A trinity of evil. They accord with the "seducing spirits," and their "doctrines of devils," that the Apostle Paul tells us of. 1. Tim. 4:1 &c. Their mission is by the specious reasoning of worldly wisdom to blind the eyes of men to the truth, and to harden their hearts against the God of heaven. The Beast and the False Prophet are their agencies.

*Lu. 18:7-8. Rev. 6:11.

V. 14. "*That great day of God Almighty.*"
This day is to be carefully distinguished
from "the coming of the Lord." That has
taken place already. It was for his people.*
They are now (at this stage of the prophetic
history) with him on Mount Sion, spectators
of these earthly judgments. The day of the
Lord is his coming for vengeance. These
tribulations are only the preludes to it. Cf.
Mal. 4: Joel, 2: 2. Thess. 1:7, &c.

"*To gather them*" *&c.* Cf. Joel, 3:9, &c.
Ezek. 38:39: Dan. 12:1. Zech. 12:14:

In Ezek. 38: and 39: the Revisers read:
"Son of Man, set thy face toward Gog,
of the land of Magog, the prince of Rosh
(רֹאשׁ), Meshech, and Tubal, &c." (V. 2).
Meshech may stand for Moscow, and Tubal
for Tobalsk.

The "Gog" mentioned here (Ezek. 38, 2),
is not to be confounded with the "Gog" of
Rev. 20:8. The two struggles may be
wrapped up in this prophecy of Ezekiel. But
this up-rising of 16:14† is to be introductory
to the millennium, that of Chp. 20: will be
after, and just before the final judgment.

V. 15. This reads like a parenthesis. The
R. V. marks it as such. It is the oft re-

---

*2. Thess. 2:1. And 1. Thess. 4:13, &c. †Cf. 17:12–15.
And 19: 19.

peated warning of the Master, and it is always addressed to his Church.* True and faithful ones, will then, as now, be found in every portion of the visible Church.

The Seer's attention is for a moment diverted from the onward movement of the vision, to receive this message from his Lord, that he may write, and hand it down† to the Church,‡ It is intended especially for the Church of that day—the woman hiding in the wilderness. It will not only be a source of warning, but of hope and cheer to the remnant of the seed in this their hour of great perplexity and distress.

"*Keepeth his garments.*" Cf. 3:18.

V. 16. The movement of the vision is resumed. "*And he gathered*" &c. The revisers translate—"they." This is better. The reference then would be to the "three unclean spirits" of V. 13—"and they gathered, &c." "*Armagedon.*" More correctly Har-Magedon. Har, signifies mountain. Some have fancied that they can locate the spot. It is certain that this battle-field will not be far distant from Jerusalem.

V. 17. "*The seventh angel poured out his vial, &c.*" It is the last. The 7th seal unfolded into the seven trumpets, and the sev-

enth trumpet into the seven vials. But there is
no unfolding for the seventh vial. There are
no more developments. This is the end.
"It is done." A cry once went up from the
cross—"It is finished." That death and
that cry were great mysteries. But they
were only a part of the one great mystery of
sin. That, too, is now finished. "It is
done." The full measure of divine judgment is meted out. The last drop in the
cup once filled with wrath has been poured
out, and the very dregs thereof the wicked
of the earth have wrung out and drank,* The
result is that the earth is a wreck. Its physical conditions are disturbed; its governments
have ceased to be; its social order and commerce are broken up; and multitudes of its
inhabitants are slaughtered. Those that remain are terror stricken, and their hearts failing them for fear of what may be coming.
Satan and the two Beasts have not yet been
judged. They are still on the earth, and
now realize fully their defeat and coming
doom. But one more event is waited for. The
Lord is at hand indeed. Not only heaven,
but earth and hell now regard it as certain.

Just at this point there is again an interruption in the onward movement of the

*Ps. 75:8.

drama, and it extends through Chps. 17: and 18:   The object of this interruption is to show the Seer the results of the out-pouring of these vials—to let him see as it were, the wreckage.

REVELATION 17:

Act IV.   11:15 &c. to 20: 1-4.
Scene, 6th.   Chps. 17. 18:
Location.   The earth.
Dramatis Personæ. The   Harlot.   The Sea Beast.   The ten Kings.   The explaining Angel.
Time.   At the end of Daniel's week, after the pouring out of the last vial, and just prior to the Parousia.

The first object to which the seer's attention is called is "the great Harlot that sitteth upon many waters," and the judgment upon her. That he may the better understand who this woman is, and how her judgment is brought about, the explaining Angel takes him back a little in the order of events. At the beginning of the career of the sea-Beast and of the ten Kings, or Kingdoms,* this Harlot had long been enticing and debauching the nations. For centuries

---

*13:1, &c., 17:12,

she had been drunk with the blood of the saints, and had been making the inhabitants of the earth drunk with the wine of her fornication.

The sea-Beast—the "symbol of the aggregate of the empires of this world as opposed to Christ," as we learn from 13:3 and 17:8, receives a wound unto death, and for a while is not. But his wound is healed, and he is again. It was suggested that this wounding to death was the wiping out of all social order and monarchical forms of government, by means of socialism, communism, etc.* Out of the chaotic state that will follow, the Beast of the sea, the eighth head, would arise. The Harlot woman (the Apostate Church) will be the first to welcome him, and to assist him in grasping the reins of government and in restoring order. For this assistance the Beast and the ten Kings will for a while be very grateful, and will carry the woman—will enrich her, and sustain her in her assumptions and aggrandizements. As they acquire power, however, and progress in their sacriligious claims and blasphemies, they will realize that the woman is in their way and troublesome, and too much of a burden to carry. They will therefore turn

*See p. 165, &c.

against her and hate her.* And thus it comes to pass, according to the Angel, that the ten horns and the Beast are of one mind in hating, and in destroying the woman.

V. 1. "*I will show unto thee,*" &c. It was one of the seven vial-angels. He had already executed his office. The judgment was a thing of the past.

" *The great Harlot*" (R. V.). A woman † is almost exclusively the symbol of the Church, and a harlot—an adulterous woman, of an Apostate Church. Jer. 2:3: Ezek. 16:23: Hos. 1:3: 2 Cor. 11:2. Cf. Eph. 5:25-27. Num. 25:1, &c. Cf. Rev. 2:14.

"*Many waters.*" Cf. V. 15. Her existence and power rests upon the ignorance and superstitions of many peoples. The Roman and Greek Churches number at the present time fully 250,000,000.

V.3. "*The Wilderness*" is here equivalent to, and is explained by the "many waters" of Vs. 1 and 15. The expression is used in this sense in Ezek. 20:35, 36. God says to Israel—"I will bring you into the Wilderness of the people," &c. If this is the correct interpretation, then the Seer must be understood as saying—he (the Angel) gave me spiritual comprehension to perceive (take

---

*17:16.   †See p. 143.

in) Kingdoms, and great masses of peoples*
who had been inveigled into the meshes of
this Harlot, and who were sustaining her.

"*I saw a woman sitting upon a scarlet-
colored Beast,*" i. e., up-borne, sustained by
him.   This is a formidable combination.
The Beast, and the ten Kings, and the great
Harlot—the God-defying World-power, and
the Apostate Church, in confederation.   It
has long existed.   It exists now, and will
continue during this dispensation.   The
fowls of the air have taken possession of the
tree that had spread its branches to heaven.
Yea, the Woman herself mixed her meal
with the unholy leaven, until the whole became leavened.†   But the Witnesses for the
sufferings of Jesus, and the glory to follow,
must neither be surprised nor discouraged at
the successes of the one, nor because of the
God-defying assumptions of the other.   Their
time is coming.

The position, outward adornments, and
atrocious doings, of this woman, point un-
questionably to the Church of Rome. E. g.
Her arrayment in purple, etc. (V. 4.)   The
word "*Mystery*" on her forehead (V. 5).
We have it on good authority that this word
was once inscribed on the pope's tiara.‡

---

*Matt. 4:8.   †Matt. 13:31-34.   ‡Lange on Rev. p. 309.

"*Mother of Harlots.*" She styles herself "Rome, Mother and Mistress." "*Drunken with the blood of the Saints,*" sets forth her merciless fury in shedding the blood of God's people.

And yet we are not to regard this "great Harlot" as exclusively Rome. In its totality, "corrupt, lifeless Christendom is the harlot." Her assumptions, power, and savage blood-thirstiness, have given Rome the unenviable prominence as the apostate Church— "THE MOTHER OF HARLOTS." As the woman in Chp. 12: stood for the true (the invisible) Church, bearing her Man-child that is caught up to God, and still continuing in the world with the remnant of her seed persecuted by satanic power; so this woman symbolizes "the unfaithful Church generally and universally" in its apostasy, and affiiliation with the Antichristian power. It is not only the Roman, but the Greek Church, and those Protestant Churches that affiliate with them in their ecclesiastical views. Because of her prominence, Rome is made to stand for the whole apostasy. It will be a unit in lending itself to the sea-Beast and the ten Kings; and up to a certain point it will be an all important factor in promoting their designs.

This confederacy is of long standing, and this united action in carrying out satanic purpose against the woman's seed at this special time, finds illustration and foreshadowing in the Lord's day, when the visible (the Jewish) Church leagued itself with Gentile power to " cut off " Messiah.

"*A scarlet colored Beast.*" This is the same with 13:1, &c.

V. 5. "*Mystery.*" The Revisers in their margin propose this reading—"and upon her forehead a name written, a mystery, BABYLON THE GREAT," etc. Lange * gives a similar rendering—"on her forehead she has a name written *as a* mystery, i.e., whosoever is able to read the name, will read the following inscription: " Babylon," etc. This reading of the passage seems to be the correct one, judging from the symbolic use of the word throughout this book.

" *Babylon.*" Babel or Babylon, confusion. The name takes us back a long way, even to the plains of Shinar.† Here we have the first record of an high-handed act of open apostasy and rebellion against the Most High. It is the beginning of worldly assumption and rebellion.‡ Babel soon develops into Babylon. And so Babylon from being the seat, became the symbol of worldliness, and of the Antichristian power.

---

*On Rev., p. 307. †Gen. 11: ‡Gen. 10: 9, 10.

This Harlot woman (the Apostate Church) is given this name; because (1) she would (as known by the spirit of prophecy) identify herself with this God-defying Gentile-power; because (2) she would possess the city (Rome), which at the time the vision was given, was the successor of Babylon as the capital of this world-power; because (3) it was from her (all through the iron and clay period of this power) that these kingdoms would derive the cohesion and the strength to enable them to maintain their positions, and to dominate over the peoples and nations; because (4) she would be ever interfering with and influencing the policy and politics of these kingdoms; because (5), assuming the spiritual power to be superior to the temporal, and by this means controlling the consciences of the masses (V. 15), she would be enabled to enforce her claims, and thus would be, as she is to-day, a powerful factor in the midst of these world-governments.   Hence the statement of V. 18, " The woman which thou sawest is that great city, which reigneth over the *kings* of the earth."

She is called "that *great* city," possibly to designate her from the Babylon of the world-power, because of the heinousness of her apostasy and the magnitude of her claims.   The Lord says: " My kingdom is not of this world." She says: "It is." And in his name, she has made herself empress of the world, reigning over the kings of the earth, and domineering the con- sciences of men.

"*The Mother of Harlots.*" This clearly implies that she (the Roman Church) is not alone. It gives her pre-eminence over the others, and she is made to stand for all. The Revisers translate: "The mother of *the* har- lots, and *of the* abominations," etc.

V. 6. "*I wondered with great admira- tion*"—"with great wonder," (R. V.) The seer recognizes the symbol (a woman) as that of the Church. Perhaps he recalls her as he had last seen her in Chp. 12, and he is therefore amazed at her present appearance, "drunken with the blood of the saints, and with the blood of the martyrs of Jesus, and identified with the blasphemous Beast.

Vs. 8–14. We have identified this Beast with the sea-Beast of Chp. 13, and for our explanation of these verses, see p. 159, &c.

V. 9. "*Here is the mind which hath wis- dom.*" Wisdom not of this world, but which cometh from above. We are reminded of Daniel, 12:4, 9, 10. It is a note of explana- tion and warning intended for the Lord's people who shall be on the earth when these developments come about. His people will be found then, as now, hidden away in all the Churches, and to their enlightened minds the call will be understood and appreciated.

V. 14. *"These shall make war with the Lamb."* It must be through the remnant of the Woman's seed. Here is the only way that they can strike at the Lamb. The statement helps us to the reason why these powers should turn against the Harlot who had been so helpful to them. In striking at the Harlot, they thought they were warring against the Lamb. But it is a case of mistaken identity. This woman was a fraud. She was a wretched caricature of the followers of the Lamb—"the called, and chosen, and faithful." Still, in her outward forms, and in her spiritual assumptions, she was a reminder of Him, and in so far was a hindrance. They hated him and therefore must hate everything that reminded them of Him. "The remnant" were scattered and hidden away. They could only be attacked and slaughtered as individuals. But this woman is ostentatiously visible. She "sitteth upon many waters," and in her corporate capacity she is accessible to those who hate her.

V. 16. The Beast and ten horns are the instruments in the execution of this judgment. This, of course, is prior to their being overcome by the Lamb.   Note the four elements of destruction.

1.   They "make her desolate"—by withdrawing the support of the secular arm.

2.   They make her "naked"—they strip her of her false claims and they expose her frauds, and take from her all her spiritual offices.

3.   They "eat her flesh"—her substance —her ill-gotton wealth, and divide it among themselves.

4.   They "burn her with fire."   Lange says:* " In a sarcastic *auto da fé*, suggestive of so many like proceedings" in her drunken rage against God's children.

And so the Lord spues the Apostate Church out of his mouth.†

V. 17.   *"For God hath put it into their hearts to fulfil his will,"* &c.   God's grasp upon his government is never relaxed.   The heathen may rage, and the people imagine a vain thing, and the Kings of the earth set themselves up, and the rulers take counsel together, and that, too, against the Lord; but his bit is in their mouths.   They cannot lift a finger, or take a step, without his permission.   Nay, more, he orders and controls all their action.   And when they think them-

---

*On Rev., p. 309,   †3:16.

selves most free and most wise, and most independent, then it is that they are but instruments in accomplishing the good pleasure of his will. And yet they are free. What they do, they do from the heart, and with a will. In this instance we are told "these shall hate the Harlot." The destruction they brought upon her was wholly in accordance with their own desires, and for the accomplishment of their own purposes. But Jehovah God, the God whom they had denied and blasphemed, was also accomplishing his purposes. Howbeit they mean not so, neither do their hearts think so. *

Just at this point in the prophetic history, and by way of review, we may notice the well organized confederacy that has been developed in this portion of the drama. †

(a) *The Dragon*, Chp. 12:3, etc. He is represented as having seven heads, etc. By this appearance Satan is identified with Gentile dominion. He has energized it through its long career, beginning with Babel and Nimrod. ‡ And so here he wears the emblems of worldly dominion. He is the power behind the throne. It is not, however, until after he has been excluded from the heavenlies and from the Divine presence,

---

*Is. 10:5, &c.   †Is. 8: 9, &c.   Rev. 16: 13, 14.   ‡Gen. 10:9, 10.

and has come down to the earth,* that he takes human shape, and gives his power, etc. †
to a man.   His destiny is given us in Chp. 20:10.

(*b*)   *The Beast* — the sea-Beast. ‡   His destiny is recorded in Chp. 19:20.   He is not killed, but taken, and cast alive into a lake of fire.   All prophetic language points to special judgment upon the Antichrist.§

(*c*) "The ten Horns," or Kingdoms, out of which the sea-Beast is to arise, and which will give their power and strength to him.‖ Their destiny is given us in Chps. 16:14, and 19:17, etc.

(*d*) "*Another Beast*"—the earth-Beast.¶ He is the same as the False-Prophet.** His destiny is united with that of the sea-Beast.††

(*e*) "*The great Harlot.*"‡‡ For her destiny see 17:16, etc.

CHAPTER 18:

There is much unanimity in the interpretation of the symbols of these two chapters.§§ The Harlot of the one, and the Babylon of the other, are types of the apostate Church,

---

*12:9. †13:2. ‡13:1, etc. §Dan 9:27; 7:11; 8:25; 11:45.
2. Thess. 2:8; Rev. 7:11. ‖13:1, 17:12, 13. ⸜13:11.
**16:13. ††19:20. ‡‡17. §§The 17: and 18:

i. e. of Rome. Chapter 17:, it is supposed, pictures the Harlot Church, and discloses the agents of her destruction; while chapter 18: describes to us under the symbol of a city— "great Babylon," the results of this destruction.

There are very serious difficulties that call for explanation before this view can be accepted.   It is probable that no explanation can be given that will be free from difficulties, we must therefore examine and choose that which presents the least.

The statement in V. 18 (17:)—The woman which thou sawest is that great city," etc., seems strongly to favor the close connection and identity of these two chapters.   The name "Babylon the Great," that is upon the Harlot's forehead, also strengthens this view. Further, in Vs. 3, 6–9, of Chp. 18, there are expressions and allusions that tally with the descriptions and doings of the Harlot in Chp. 17, and that makes the argument all the stronger in favor of the oneness of these visions.

On the other hand, there are descriptions and facts to be noted in this 18th Chp. that can have no relation to an apostate Church, nor to the city of Rome, as its representative. They seem clearly to indicate that the visions refer to different subjects.

1. Note the fact that the chapters themselves seem to give distinct evidence to this
effect.   The agencies used in describing to the
Seer the results of the judgments are different.   Chp. 17: opens with the announcement:
"One of the seven Angels which had the
seven vials, talked with me," etc., and in
Chp. 18: the Seer says: "After these things I
saw another Angel come down from heaven,"
etc.   Here is a different agent.   He is not
even one of the seven-vialed angels.   The
conjunction "and," at the beginning of the
verse, is omitted by the Revisers, thus dis-
connecting the two visions more completely.
We seem in this way to be notified that the
vision of the Harlot is finished—that we are
done with her, and that we are now called to
the consideration of other events.

Keep in mind the situation as we are sup-
posing it.   The last vial has been poured
out.   The earth is a wreck.   The onward
movement of events has been arrested, and
the Seer has been called to look upon the
results—the debris.   The first accomplished
judgment to which his attention is directed
is that of the woman's—the Harlot's.   It is
complete.   But the woman is not the only
subject for judgment.   There are many.
There are all her confederates.   Not one will
be allowed to escape.   In Chp. 17: we are

told that she is burnt with fire—consumed utterly. There is nothing more to be said concerning her. Here ends her history. And now (Chp. 18:), after this picture of completed judgment has been exhibited, another angel comes to the Seer, and shows him, as we think, another wreck. True, he speaks of this destruction as that of "Babylon the Great" (V. 2), the name given to the apostate Church of Chp. 17:. The reason for the use of this symbol, in connection with the Harlot woman, has already been given.* This apostate Church has been so greedy after political power, and has been so successful—"reigning over the kings of the earth," that of necessity she becomes identified in spirit and in action with the world-power. Consequently the language that is descriptive of the one is also applicable to the other. Thus we can readily reconcile the fact that these two chapters treat of different subjects, although using descriptive language that in several instances is identical.

2. Note also that while in Chp. 17: the Harlot is spoken of as "Babylon the Great," in Chp. 18: there is no mention made of the Harlot. The subject of this last vision is— a city, a great centre of political power and

*p. 211.

commercial influence, and if she is called "a queen," and "no widow," it is the self-assertion of her own heart. It is also the spirit and language that the O. T. Scriptures ascribe to Babylon, the imperial mistress of the world, the capital of Gentile-power at that time.* All her surroundings are materialistic — merchantmen, ships, commerce, slaves, all kinds of merchandise, enriching herself and others. Very different from this is the woman in Chp. 17: She wears the gorgeous apparel, but she does not sell it, and even where they seem to have things in common there is a difference. *E. g.* The inhabitants of the earth are said to have been made drunk with the wine of the Harlot's fornication;† but of this city it is announced that, the nations have drank of the wine of the *wrath* of her fornification (18:3). In the first instance it is the picture of feasting and debauchery, delightful to the animal man; in the other, it is the participation in the judgments inflicted.‡

3. The statement V. 24 (18:) is not strictly true of the Harlot of Chp. 17:; but it is of Babylon as the symbol of Gentile dominion. Rome, as an Apostate Church, has for the most part used the secular arm

---

*Is. 13:19. 14:4. 47:1, &c. Zeph. 2:15. †17:2. ‡Rev. 14:10.

in her murders.   Whereas this world-power
has not only slaughtered God's people that
have been handed over to it, but multitudes
that cannot be charged to Rome.   In regard
to this power it can truly be said—"and in
her was found the blood of prophets, and of
saints, and of all that were slain upon earth."
The devil was a murderer from the beginning.*

4.   Then observe that in Chp. 17: the
Beast and the ten Kings hate the woman.
They are of one mind in desiring her destruction, and are the willing instruments in its
accomplishment.   Not so in the destruction
of the Babylon of Chp. 18:   Neither the
Beast, nor the ten Kings are the instruments,
of it.   They do not desire it.   On the contrary, they mourn over it.   Kings (V. 9), as
well as merchants, bewail her.

5.   And observe further, that this lamen-
tation by representatives of commerce, never
has been, and never can be, applicable over
the destruction of an Apostate Church, nor
over the City of Rome, as its representative.
Rome has never been a commercial city. Her
situation is against it, and the lack of states-
manship has ever driven from her gates the
commerce that might have drifted towards it.

---

*John, 8;14,

6. And once more let it be noted that while in the 17th chapter the agents of the woman's punishment, and the manner of it, are carefully given; in Chp. 18th, all such information is with-held. The intimation is that it is sudden—"in one hour,"* and we are left to the inference that it is effected without human agency. If man had accomplished her ruin, "the Kings of the earth would have been the agents most forward in the movement; but we read that they are among her chief mourners.

In view of these considerations, we are disposed to regard the Babylon of Chp. 18th, as the symbol of the Babylon of the Euphrates. As such, it stands for the civilization and dominion of Gentile power, At the time of this overthrow, it may have been centralized, as in the days of Nebuchadnezzar. Perhaps after the destruction of the Harlot by the Beast, Rome may be made the capital of his ursurpations, of his commerce, and of his idolatrous practices. We are not, however, so much disposed to regard it as the destruction of a city, as of a system. Babylon represents the whole succession of Gentile dominion in the culmination of its power, its culture, its prosperity, and its

---

*Vs. 10, 19,

wickedness. It is the world full-ripe for judgment. It is the great metallic image standing on its feet, and the stone crashing against it, and toppling it over, and grinding it to powder.

Any difficulties that may be suggested by expressions found, *e. g.* in Vs. 3, 6, 9, 18, will be readily removed, by keeping before us the fact that this world-empire will have assumed at this time an ecclesiastical character. Like the Apostate Church, it has become a politico-ecclesiastical power. Its head is the Anti-Christ. He has assumed divine prerogatives and honors. He has his false-prophet, and performs miracles, and makes merchandise—not only of gold, but of "souls of men," sealing them with his mark, and compelling them to worship him.

V. 2. The language of this verse is that of the O. T. scriptures.* It was the prophetic denunciation against the Babylon of that day. It is now the announcement of the fulfillment of these denunciations upon the whole world-system of which Babylon was then the embodiment.

The angel speaks of this judgment as a thing accomplished—"Babylon is fallen"—"is become," etc.

---

*Is. 13:21, 22; 34:11, 13–15. Jer. 50;51.

V. 20. The whole face of things is now changed. The world's day of rejoicing is past. The sorrow of God's people is about to be turned into joy. The waiting time for the souls under the altar is at an end.* The assurance given to his Church by the Lord in the days of his flesh, is on the eve of accomplishment—"I will see you again, and your heart shall rejoice, and your joy no man taketh from you."†

REVELATION 19.

Act IV. 11:15, etc., to 20:1—4.
Scene 7th. Chps. 19:20: 1–4.
Location. Heaven and Earth.
Dramatis Personæ. The King of Kings. The Bride. The Living Ones. The Elders. The Armies of Heaven. The Beast and False-Prophet. Kings of the earth. Satan.
Time. "The End."

The onward movement of events is now resumed. It was interrupted, as suggested, at the close of Chp. 17: that the wreck, produced by the vial judgments, might be exhibited to the Seer. There had been vast

---

*Rev. 6:9, etc. †John 16:20, 22.

destruction, yet there is much life remaining on the earth.   The Harlot has been burnt, and the great emporium of the world's power, and commerce, and culture, has been thrown down;* but the Antichrist and his False-Prophet are still alive and defiant.   The ten kings and their armies, and the merchants and their followers that raised so pitious a cry over their fallen Babylon, these all remain, and their judgment is at hand (19:19, etc.).

We have seen that there were three explanatory pictures given us just after the sounding of the 7th trumpet,† and just prior to the out-pouring of the vials.   The course of the prophetic history is arrested to give them.

1.   The first is that of the true (the invisible) Church, the translation of the Man-Child, and Satan cast down to earth, and persecuting the remnant of her children.‡

2.   Next we have the rise and career of the two Beasts.§

3.   And then comes the picture of the Lamb and his 144,000, on Mount Sion—the once invisible and struggling Church, now translated and amid the heavenly glories.

These are the three pictures explanatory of the situation at the beginning of the last half

---

*17:16; 18:21.   †11:15.   ‡12:   §13:

of Daniel's week, and just before the pouring out of the vial judgments.

Chapter 15th takes us back to the initial scene of the triumphal song of the opened temple.* And Chp. 16th tells us of the going forth of the angels with their vials, and of the judgments that are executed. Once again, we have the history interrupted, but only for a moment, that the Seer may have the opportunity of surveying the ruin that has been produced—the destruction of the Harlot—the false Church; and the over-throw of Babylon, the center of the world's commerce, civilization, and power.

And now, in Chp. 19:, we are called back to the Mount Sion scene of Chp. 14:. That scene was just after the translation, and just before the pouring out of the vials. This (19:) is after the wrath has expended itself. The scene is in the heavens. The "much people" of V. 1. (the Redeemed), have been lookers-on at all these dreadful events. These are they who have been counted worthy to escape all those things that have come upon the earth.† They are the "called, and the chosen, and the faithful."‡ They heard the voice bidding them in Chp. 18:20, "rejoice over her," etc. And now we have the response:

---

*11:15;etc.   †Lu. 21:36.   ‡17:14.

"A great voice of much people in heaven, saying, Alleluia! Salvation, and glory, and honour, and power, unto the Lord our God," etc.

And so this 7th scens opens. It is the last grand scene that brings this present dispensation to its close. With Chp. 19th, the movement of the prophetic history is resumed, and is not again interrupted until it reaches its glorions consummation.

V. 1.   This is the same multitude that has been brought to our notice before in Chps. 7:9, and 14:1, &c.

There is a two-fold cause for the halleluias. (a) The destruction of the Harlot, (V. 2.) and (b) the marriage of the Lamb, (V. 6.)

V. 3.   *"And her smoke rose up forever and ever."* Alas, for the fastidious preachers ·of our day who cannot so much as say— "hell fire."   They will hardly be able to join in the halleluias of this rejoicing people!

V. 4.   The first portion of this chapter · is a grand, responsive choral service. The first three verses are the response of the Redeemed to the summons in Chp. 18:20.   In this verse (4) the Living Ones, and the Elders, worship, and respond, with their— "amen, alleluia," to the anthems of the Redeemed.   It is the same *Throne* scene so magnificently pictured in Chp. 4th. After this (V. 5.) there comes a voice from out of *The Throne* calling upon all the servants of God to praise him, and then is heard the grand chorus from "a great multitude, as the voice of many waters, and as the voice of mighty thunderings, saying, alleluia! For the Lord God Omnipotent reigneth (V. 6.)

V. 7. "*The marriage of the Lamb,*" &c. The Bride is the whole body of the Re-deemed at the time of the Lord's second com-ing; and "the marriage is the union of this body with a personally present Christ in glory and government."* Another picture of this event is given in Dan. 7:13, &c., and still another in Rev. 20:4.

"*His wife.*" We have called attention to the fact that throughout the Apocalypse a woman is the symbol of the Church, and that as such it has a three fold sense.

1.   The woman of Chp. 12:, is the true, pure Church.   It is the little flock;† the Be-lievers of all ages;‡ the sealed ones;§ the faith-ful witnesses on earth, the "called, and chosen, and faithful;"‖ "the blessed company of all faithful people."

2.   The woman of Chp. 17th is the visi-ble Church.   She has become a Harlot, apostate, unfaithful to her Lord and spouse.

---

*E. R. C. in Lange, p. 337.   †Lu. 12:32.   ‡Heb. 11: §Rev. 7: ‖11: 17:14.

3.   The woman of Chp. 19: 7, and 21:9,
is the same as at Chp. 12.   It is the faithful
Church now glorified—the Bride of the
Lamb; the wife, partaking of the marriage
feast.

The woman, the Harlot, the Bride.   These
are the three aspects of the Church as presented to us in the New Testament.   The
woman is the Church Militant, the Bride is
the Church triumphant*

"*Hath made herself ready.*"   "These are
they which have come out of great tribulation, and have washed their robes, and made
them white in the blood of the Lamb."†

V. 8.   Note the contrast between the
simple dress of the Bride, and the vulgar
gorgeousness of the Harlot.‡

"*The fine linen is the righteous acts of
the saints.*" (R. V.)   It is their own righteousness, that which is inherent, as distinct
from that which is imputed.§

V. 9.   "*The marriage supper.*"   It was
promised long ago—"I will not drink henceforth of this fruit of the wine, until that day
when I drink it new with you in my Father's
kingdom."‖   "That day" has now come.

---

*Auberlin, p. 276.†   Rev. 7:14.   22:14.   Jude, 24.
Eph. 3:20.   5:25, &c.   ‡17:4.   §Alford in loco.   ‖Matt.
26:29.   ¶10:4.

"*Write.*" This is in contrast with "seal up those things," &c. ¶

V. 10. "*And I fell down before his feet to worship him, and he said unto me, see thou do it not: I am a fellow servant,*" (R. V). Clearly there is no saint worship in the Church above.

V. 11. Thus far everything has been preparatory. It may be that while the vials are being poured out upon the earth, these events are transpiring in heaven. While earth is being convulsed to its centre, the Marriage of the Lamb with his Bride is taking place in heaven with appropriate festivities and rejoicings, the armies of the King are gathering, and the King himself is preparing to go forth in righteousness to judge and to make war. And now the last vial is drained, and the Seer has beheld the wreckage. All is ready, and—heaven opens. It had opened on the Christ in his humiliation that his divine sonship might be recognized;* it had opened for his readmission as the risen savior;† and now it opens for him again, that he may go forth as King of Kings, and Lord of Lords.

In Chp. 4th, V. 1, it is a door that is

---

*Matt. 3:16.   †Acts, 1:9, 11.   ‡Rev. 1:7.   Ps. 68: 1–5, 17, 32, &c.

opened. Here it is heaven itself. Heaven's King with heaven's armies is to pass out, and a door is not sufficient. Heaven itself must open to give him egress. ‡

V. 13. "*His name is . . The word of Goa.*" John, 1:1, and 1. John 1:1.

"*Clothed in a vesture dipped in blood.*" Is. 63:1, &c.

V. 14. "*And the armies in heaven followed him,*" etc. Matt 25:31 &c.

This is Jesus glorified. He is no longer the despised Galilean, the homeless wanderer, the man that has not where to lay his head, the rejected Messiah, the crucified malefactor; but the exalted Prince and Savior, going forth with the shout of a king. Heaven, earth, and hell are stirred at his presence. Every eye is attracted to him. Enemies tremble before him. Believers admire his beauty and rejoice in him. The whole universe is astir with interest, and adds pomp and magnificence to the occasion. And this is Jesus. He who once hung on the cross, with the inscription written over him in mockery—"*The King of the Jews.*" All is now changed. By the Divine decree, he is exalted head over all things, and he goes forth from the midst of the very THRONE itself with the names emblazoned on his vesture—King of Kings and Lord of Lords.

Every eye in the universe beholds him, every tongue confesses to him, every knee bows before him. And this is Jesus again with us—Jesus in the glory foreshadowed on the mount.

Up to this point (V. 14) it is an heavenly picture. Now the triumphal march begins, and the scene is transferred to earth.

V. 15. "*Out of his mouth goeth a sharp sword,*" *&c.** It is the sharp sword of judicial decision.†

V. 17. "*Standing in the Sun,*" as this proclaiming Angel does, possibly denotes his conspicuousness. This is that day and hour of which it was once said—no man knoweth; no, nor the angels of heaven, but my Father only.‡ It is now so proclaimed, and in such "a loud voice," throughout the great universe, that even the very fowls that fly in the midst of heaven are summoned to be present, and to take part in its awful events.

"*The supper of the great God.*" This is in marked contrast with the Marriage Supper of the Lamb (V. 9).

There is a similar summons in Ezekiel (39:17–21). His prophecy in chapters 37: to 40:, clearly synchronizes with this time, and

---

*2. Thess. 2:8. Hos. 6:5. †Matt. 25:31, &c. ‡Matt. 24:36.

will be found profitable reading in this connection.   It fills out what is here only in
outline.   The destruction of the Anti-christ
and his host, the restoration of Juda and
Israel, and the King who is to reign over
them in righteousness,—these are the subjects on which the prophet dwells with
remarkable fulness.

V. 19.   For the preparations on the part
of the Beast for the conflict, see 16:14, 16
and 17:8-16.

Vs. 20, 21.   This is the consummation
determined.   It is poured out on the desolator.*   He is the Prince of the people that
should come, after the cutting off of Messiah,
to destroy the holy City; he is the man of
sin, the son of perdition, of the Epistle†; and
he is the Beast of the Apocalypse and of
Daniel.‡

CHAPTER 20:1-4.

Of the great confederacy to which we have
called attention,§ we have seen the Harlot
burned with fire, the ten Kings and their
armies slain with the sword, the two Beasts
taken and cast alive into the lake of fire, and

---

*Dan. 9:27.   †2. Thess. 2:8.   ‡Rev. 13:1 &c. and Dan
7:11.   §p. 216.

now there remains but one to be dealt with
—Satan, the head and front of this rebellion.
The first verses of this 20th chapter tell us
what is done with him. He is bound, and
cast into the bottomless pit, and shut in, that
he should deceive the nations no more, till
the thousand years should be fulfilled.

Act V.   20:4-7.

Scene 1st.—Chp. 20:4-7.

Location.—The earth.

Dramatis Personæ.—Christ; they that are
his—resurrected; and the inhabitants of the
earth.

Time.—The times of refreshment and
restoration of all things.

These are the times of refreshing and of
the restoration of all things, "which God
hath spoken by the mouth of all his prophets
since the world began."*   It is Jesus, the son
of the Highest upon the throne of his father
David,† and his saints about him.‡   This is
the time of Israel's redemption and glory.
The seventy weeks determined upon the people and the holy city have now met their
accomplishment.   Transgression is finished;
an end has been made of sins; reconciliation

---

*Acts 3:19 &c.   †Lu. 1:32.   ‡Matt. 19:28. Dan.
7:13 &c.

for iniquity has been accomplished; everlasting righteousness has been brought in; the
visions and the prophecy have been ratified;
and the Most Holy has been anointed.* If
we would know more of the splendor of this
reign than is here given, we must study the
"sure word of prophecy" that we have concerning it.

V. 4. "*Judgment was given unto them.*"
The Lord and his saints reigning.† At his
coming the Lord subdues, judges, and pun-
ishes‡—he treads "the wine-press of the
fierceness and wrath of Almighty God,"
and then brings in his salvation and estab-
lishes his kingdom in righteousness. The
little Stone becomes a great Mountain. The
proclamation goes forth, and the kingdom of
this world becomes the kingdom of our God
and his Christ. It probably will be theo-
cratic, such as Israel's was at the first. Jesus
is king. His is the throne. The government is on his shoulders. But saints and
men will be the agents in the administration.
Thus Jesus will reign over the earth, but not
necessarily upon it. Perhaps his relations
to the earth may be shadowed forth by the
transfiguration scene.§ His position was on

---

*Dan. 9:24; see p. 26. †Dan. 7:13, 14, 27. ‡Matt.
25:31 &c. §Matt. 17:

the mount, and thus above the earth and overlooking it; and disciples, men in the flesh, representatives of the earth and its kingdom, prostrate at his feet. The heavenly and the earthly brought together, yet separate and distinct. Men in glory, and men in the flesh, and Jesus visible to all, accepted by all, and controling all. And, to fill up to completeness the typical scene, from the throne of his glory—the mount of eminence, He shall be transfigured before men, and glorified saints, and angels; and the voice from the most excellent glory, penetrating through all space, and heard by all Intelligences, shall announce—"This is my beloved Son, in whom I am well pleased. Hear ye Him."

"*Thrones, and they sat upon them.*" Who are "they?" Undoubtedly the sealed ones of Chp. 7th, and the 144,000 of Chp. 14th. They are the Redeemed of all ages—both those who have slept in Jesus, and those who were caught up to meet him at his coming.

"*And I saw the souls of them that were beheaded.*" *&c.* And who are these? Do they differ from them who sat on the thrones? The inference seems to be that they do. Who then are they? We have accounted for the resurrected in Christ, and for the translated. They are on the "thrones." After the "Man-child" was caught up to God, the woman still continued on the earth, and it was "the remnant of her seed" that was to contend with the Beast, and to refuse to receive his mark, and to worship his image, and that must witness for Jesus, even unto death.* And these must be they. " The souls of them that were beheaded for the witness of Jesus, and for the word of God, and which had not worshiped the Beast, neither his image, neither had received his mark upon their foreheads, or in their hands." The foolish virgins returned with oil in their lamps. It was too late for the marriage feast. The door was already shut. They must abide without, and face the storm; and by keeping the commandments of God, and maintaining the testimony of Jesus, amid the universal Apostacy, they must make amends for past unfaithfulness, and they too shall live and reign with Christ a thousand years.

V. 5. "*The rest of the dead,*" i. e., those not included in the above category.

"*A thousand years.*" We are not compelled to restrict this to literal years. "One day is with the Lord as a thousand years, and a thousand years as one day."† It sym-

---

*12:17.   †2. Pet. 3:8.

bolizes an æon—the world's sabbatic year, an age of blessedness.

"*This is the first resurrection.*" Scripture speaks of three resurrections. In the 15th Chp. of 1. Cor., the Apostle presents the fact of a resurrection, and says (V. 22): "For as in Adam all die, even so in Christ shall all be made alive. But," he continues, "every man in his own order." And then he gives this order.

1. "Christ the first-fruits." First in pre-eminence, and in the peculiarity of its conditions; and first also in the order of time, in that there was none before, and has been none since, like it.

2. "Afterward they that are Christ's at his coming." An interval of near two thousand years has now elapsed since the Lord's resurrection, and this after-resurrection has not yet taken place. This is the resurrection that in this vision is mentioned as the first.

3. "Then"—after the resurrection of those at Christ's coming—"then the end." This will be a long interval. Not only is there the thousand years of the reign, but there is also the period of the Satanic outbreak. It is not until after this event that we read: "And I saw the dead, small and great, stand before God," &c. (V. 12), and this is "the end," or the second resurrection.

Here only two resurrections are referred to. The vision concerns things present and future—"the things which are, and the things which shall be hereafter."* The resurrection of Christ is so peculiar to himself, and is an event so entirely of the far past, that it is not brought into consideration here. The resurrections mentioned here are the same that the Lord refers to when he says that "all in the graves shall hear his voice, and shall come forth; they that have done good to the resurrection of life; and they that have done evil, unto the resurrection of judgment."† These are two distinct resurrections, and as such well defined by scripture usage. When the resurrection of the Lord, or of those in him, is the object of reference, the preposition *εκ* is always introduced, and it is a resurrection *out of*, or *from among*, the dead: But when it speaks of this last rising—the resurrection of judgment—the preposition is omitted, and its language is—the resurrection *of* the dead.

V. 6. "*The second death.*" There is no question as to the nature of this death.‡ But what is the first death? Is it merely the dissolution of the body? This seems to be the

---

*Rev. 1:19.   †John 5:28, 29. Lu. 14:14. Acts 24:15.
‡21:8,

accepted view. But is there not a prior death? A death to which we must trace the dissolution of the body? *We venture to suggest that the first death is our condition by nature—a fleshly-mind that is enmity against God. Thus antagonized the soul is "without God,"and is "condemned already." And so we read: "The mind of the flesh is death."† (R. V.)

This we take to be the first death. There is hope in it, for Christ can quicken the dead in trespasses and sins.‡ And hence the distinction so strikingly brought out here. In the first death there is hope, in the second there is none. It is "the lake of fire" burning forever and ever.§ Those who attain to this "first resurrection" are they who in this life have passed (εκ) out of (R. V.) this first death-state into the life-state.|| "On such the second death hath no power."

"The second death" is then the carrying out to the full that sentence of condemnation which is on this first death, and which has not been lifted in this life. The soul is now without hope, and is "punished with everlasting destruction from the presence of the Lord, and from the glory of his power."¶

*Rom. 5:12. James 1:14, 15. †Rom. 8:6, 7. Eph. 2:1, 11-13. ‡Eph. 2:1. John 6:40, 47, 57. 5:24. §Rev. 20:14. 21:8. 14:11. ||John 5:24. ¶2. Thess. 1:9.

REVELATION 20.

Act VI.   20:7-15.

This act may be divided into two scenes—
Scene 1st.—The Apostacy.
Scene 2d.—The Judgment.

Its location will be the earth, and its dramatis personæ will be Satan, the inhabitants of the earth, "the rest of the dead," and the Judge. The time is after the thousand years.

Vs. 7 and 8. Satan is released from his prison, and is permitted to visit the earth. At once he is at his old business—deception.* He seems not to have learned wisdom by the past. Or perhaps his fallen nature finds all its satisfaction in opposing the ways of truth and righteousness, and in leading others into sin and suffering. "The imagination of the thoughts of his heart is only evil continually."†

"Gog and Magog, to gather them together to battle." This is the last great battle with the powers of evil. After this the judgment, and the lake of fire, which is the second death.‡

The question has been asked—Why is this

---

*Gen. 3:1 &c.   †Gen. 6:5.   ‡See p. 203.

second outbreak of evil allowed? While we cannot fathom Divine counsels, we can discern a reason for this permitted outbreak, that for the present at least is abundantly satisfactory. The great problem through all these ages has been concerning evil in the universe, and its final issue. What is to be done with it? He that sits upon THE THRONE has been solving this problem. And now that He is about bringing it to its solution, he would have his wisdom perfectly apprehended, his justice fully acknowledged, and his judgments heartily acquiesced in, by all his Intelligences. To make them realize the malignant character of evil, its unalterable nature, and the exceeding danger of its presence, is an all-important step in this direction. A world is allowed to be dominated by this power. Love passing all understanding is bestowed upon it. The truth is made known to it. Grace and life are offered it. After a long and awful experience, there is given to it an æon of exemption from the curse of this power, and of blessedness in the presence of the Redeemer. In the midst of the very fulness of this blessedness, Divine influences are withdrawn, and the prince of evil is allowed once more to appear on the scene, and the heart of the fallen creature cannot stand alone. No process of training in truth and righteousness, no long continued enjoyment of paradisic bliss, can heal its hurt, or eradicate its disease. It turns at once to the intruder and welcomes his presence, and yields to his seductions. The incurable nature of this principle of evil is now completely demonstrated; and the wisdom and justice of the Sovereign Ruler of the Universe, in consigning it to everlasting destruction from the presence of his glory, is completely vindicated.

V. 10. "The lake of fire," &c. This is Gehenna. It differs from Hades and "the bottomless pit."* The Beast and False-prophet are in this lake already. And now Satan is to be cast in with his adherents, and his agencies—death and Hades. And it is forever. As he lived a thousand years in the abyss, so he and his will continue to exist in this fiery prison forever and ever. No more letting him loose to deceive and to work ruin in God's glorious universe.

And this is the end of sin, and sorrow, and death. They have their place. But God's people no more come in contact with them. For them they are things of the past. The problem of evil is solved.

---

*Rev. 19:20 &cf.c.   20:3 & 10,   Matt. 5:22, 29, 30, 10:28, Mk, 9:43,

And it must be noted that with all the events connected with this rebellion and judgment, the redeemed have no connection, save as lookers on. Their judgment has passed long, long before, and it was unto life.*
This resurrection, and the white throne, and the opened books, and the judgment, and the fiery lake—these are for those only whose names are not found written in the Lamb's book of life.

REVELATION 21:22:

Act VII.   21:22:

This introduces a new dispensation. These are "the things" in all their fulness that God has prepared for them that love him.†

Verses 24 and 28, of 1. Cor. 15: have met their accomplishment. We call attention to verses 22 to 29 of this 15th Chp. of 1. Corinthians. They are worthy of careful study. For range of thought, and condensation of statement there is nothing like it in human language. In its few paragraphs there is outlined the leading events we have been studying in this historic drama—events that

------

*John 5:29.   †1. Cor. 2:9.

in their duration and consequences, run
through all time and into the eternal ages.
Glance at them for a moment. Verse 22
tells that "in Christ shall all be made alive,"
i. e. resurrected. "But (V. 23) every man
in his own order." First, Christ. This is
redemption completed. Afterward they that
are his at his coming. This is the thousand
years of Rev. 20:"Then the end"(V. 24). The
ages of the millenium are past. The serpent's head has been crushed;* the general
resurrection and the judgment have taken
place; the devil, death and Hades have been
cast into the lake; and so, "the end"—the
completion of Messiah's work. The mystery of the Divine purposes concerning evil
has been solved. Its license has been revoked,
and its power broken, and it has been con-
signed to its own place. And what follows?
Why, He, the seed of the woman, the son
of man, David's son, delivers up the kingdom unto God, even the Father. His mission was to "destroy the works of the devil;"†
to deliver his captives from his grasp;‡ and
to restore the kingdom of this world to its
rightful sovereignty.§ And with Satan and
his emissaries (death and Hades) in the lake
of fire, his mission has been successfully

---

*Gen. 3:15.   †1. John 3:8.   ‡Eph. 4.8.   §Rev. 11:15.

accomplished. All conflict is at an end. He
has reigned "till he hath put all enemies
under his feet" (V. 26). And now a new
order of things is ordained in which God is
"all in all" (V. 28). And these are the
things that these closing chapters of the Revelation unfold to us.

V. 4. "*The former things are passed
away.*" And this passing away is not confined to things material. Things spiritual
come within its sweep. Observe, e. g., that
in the new order there is a tabernacle, i. e.
dwelling place (21:3), but no temple (V.
22). Even this is among "the former
things." The temple necessitated the priest,
the altar, and the sacrifice, This new
dispensation will not require them. The
work of redemption has been completed.
Sin, and death, and Hades, as disturbing
elements, are no more. The ruined Eden
has been restored. The instruments of that
restoration are no longer needed, and are
therefore laid aside. So also in regard to the
Messianic Kingdom. It too has accomplished its purpose, and is numbered among
the things of the past. All things have
been subdued unto the Son; and now the
Son also himself is subject unto Him that put

all things under him, that God may be all in all.*

And all things are made new (V. 4). These new things are yet in the mind and counsels of God. Secret things that belong unto Him. Even as here hinted at, they are beyond our conception and understanding. They are in the far, far away. We look toward them. In their indistinctness, they are to us as the delicate penciling of mountain ranges on the distant horizon. For more distinct outlines, and for clearer views, we must wait "until the day break, and the shadows flee away."† Meanwhile, we have a "blessed hope;" and that, too, in the near future, even "the glorious appearing," and "the kingdom;" concerning which, the Lord himself has taught us to pray, saying:

"Our Father, which art in heaven,
        .   .   .   Thy Kingdom come." Amen.

_____

*1. Cor. 15:28.   †Cant. 2:17.

www.ingramcontent.com/pod-product-compliance
Lightning Source LLC
Chambersburg PA
CBHW030817020726
47499CB00006B/1952